Irrevocable

A Curvy Girl Mafia Romance

Nichole Rose

Contents

Content Advisory	1
About the Book	2
Chapter One	4
Chapter Two	16
Chapter Three	29
Chapter Four	38
Chapter Five	51
Chapter Six	65
Chapter Seven	72
Chapter Eight	80
Chapter Nine	91
Chapter Ten	101
Chapter Eleven	111
Chapter Twelve	122
Chapter Thirteen	134

Chapter Fourteen 147

Chapter Fifteen 162

Epilogue 165

Author's Note 168

Illicit Love Series 169

The Ruined Series 171

Follow Nichole 174

Nichole's Book Beauties 176

Instalove Book Club 177

Also by Nichole Rose 178

About Nichole Rose 185

Content Advisory

Irrevocable deals with dark themes and subject matter, including murder, sexual assault (not of the FMC and not on page), and dubcon. Read at your own discretion.

About the Book

He took what didn't belong to him. Now, he'll burn it all to the ground to keep her.

Domani Brambilla

I've spent my entire life with a gun in my hand and my back against the wall.

I learned exactly two things: Kill or be killed.

That's the fate awaiting me. That's my destiny.

Right up until I find a pretty little Irish goddess asleep in a bed and take what doesn't belong to me.

Now, I'm forging my own fate and writing my own destiny.

And I intend to do it with Finley at my side.

Even if I have to wipe out every member of her family and mine to do it.

She belongs to me. Not even hell itself will take her from me now.

Finley Brennan

I've spent my entire life with a smile on my face and a cage of glass surrounding me.

I know exactly two things: My family is dangerous, and I want out.

But I never expected to be plucked from my bed by a member of the mob.

Nor did I think I'd be so ungodly attracted to him.

Domani is like no one I've ever met.

His hands are stained in blood, but when they're on my body, I don't care what kind of monster he is.

I know he's even more dangerous than my family, but I don't care about that, either.

I want him. Even if it means risking everything.

But I never expected the cost to be this high.

If love is pain, what's the price of a soul?

Chapter One

Domani

The most fucked-up nights of my life always begin the same way. Mattia Agostino, consigliere to the Valentino family, strolls in, hands in his pockets, leans against the doorframe, and says the same words.

I've got a job for you, Domani.

Once upon a time, I didn't ask many questions. It wasn't what the Valentino family paid me to do. That changed almost two years ago when the Valentino brothers—Rafe, Luca, and Gabriel—decided they were stepping back for a while, and we—Mattia, Diego Butera, Coda Passero, and I—were stepping up as the new faces of the family. It's been a fucking endless headache ever since.

But some things don't change. When Mattia says he has a job for me, I've inevitably got blood on my hands, or I'm getting stitched up by the time the sun rises.

I don't know which tonight has in store for me, but it's bound to be one or the other.

Frankly, it's a pain in my motherfucking ass. It's two in the morning. I could be sleeping right now.

But what's that saying?

Oh yeah. Life's a bitch, and then you die.

I knew what I was signing up for before I ever threw my lot in with Rafe when I was eighteen. I did what I had to do to ensure the man who raised me—my father—paid for his crimes. If my soul is black as a result, it's a small price to pay.

But if I die in Cillian Brennan's compound tonight, I'm going to be pissed about it. Being picked off by the Irish mobster and his family is not the way I want to go out.

I hoist myself over the back wall of his compound anyway, taking care not to rip my goddamn pants all to hell.

The back of his property is mired in shadow, not a single light burning in the rundown mansion. But thanks to the streetlights and the full moon, I see enough. Cars litter the backyard, some on blocks, some in various stages of being stripped. Entire patches of grass are MIA, leaving behind nothing but mudholes.

For a motherfucker worth his weight in gold, Cillian hasn't used a cent of it to restore this place since he set up shop in Chicago. It's a good front if he's trying to look like he isn't worth damn near as much as Rafe, the *capo dei capi*, I'll give him that. Unfortunately for him, no one who knows him buys it. The Irish mob has deep pockets, and Cillian is growing too powerful in this city.

It's bad for business. But we can't kill him outright. That'd spark a war we don't want. Instead, I'm bugging his fucking house. Cillian is as dirty as they come. He spends as much time fucking over his own people as he does expanding their operations. Once we get what we need, we'll pass it along and let his people handle him for us. The move is beneath us, but it's infinitely better than dragging the city back to the brink of war. We've been there far too often lately.

Granted, I have to make it into and out of this shithole first. But nothing ventured, nothing gained, and all that bullshit.

I push off from the wall, landing on my feet in the backyard. I crouch in the shadows, waiting for several long moments to see if the noise brings anyone out of the house. Nothing moves.

Huh. Interesting.

I check the gun strapped to the small of my back and the other hidden in the holster at my side and then double-check the knife in the sheath at my wrist. I've got another in a sheath at my ankle and another strapped to my thigh.

A motherfucker won't ever catch me unprepared. Been there, done that.

Satisfied that my shit is in order, I slip through the shadows, making my way closer to the house. I stop every few feet to reassess, making sure that no one has stepped out and that no one else is moving through the shadows. It takes all of ten minutes to make it to the back door. It's still dead silent inside and out.

I spot the camera aimed toward the door and quickly decide to find another route into the house. None of the windows downstairs are unlocked, and I can't risk breaking the fucking glass, but there's a window on the second floor around the side of the house that's thrown wide open.

Fuck my life. Looks like I'm climbing.

I wedge myself between a tree and the house, using both to help haul my big ass up toward the window. It doesn't take long to scale the tree, but I don't breathe the entire fucking time, worried that I'm going to place my foot wrong and go crashing down or draw attention from whoever might be in the room upstairs. There's a reason why men my size don't climb trees. When you're six-four and two hundred eighty pounds, climbing a goddamn tree isn't easy.

But I manage to haul myself to the window ledge and peer into the bedroom on the other side. Unlike the outside of the house, the bedroom is steeped in luxury. Feminine furniture and plush rugs fill the room.

The room isn't dark like I thought. The TV is on, but it's cycled back to the screen saver. The light from it washes across the four-poster bed, illuminating the woman sleeping dead center.

I stop breathing as my gaze lands on her.

Long red hair spills in waves across the pillows. Alabaster skin and soft pink lips turn my cock to steel. The covers are pushed back as if she's hot, and one arm is thrown off the side of the bed. Her nipples press against her tight little top. It ends just below her breasts, leaving her round belly exposed. She isn't wearing shorts. Just an innocent pair of pink panties. I see the lips of her pussy through them, and the urge to taste her is powerful.

Every inch of her thick, curvy body is pale and smooth, beckoning me to come closer and take what doesn't belong to me. I ache to do just that. To slip into the bed beside this beautiful little queen and know her man to woman.

I crave her. Her lips. Her breasts. The hard little nipples hiding behind that tiny shirt. The warmth spreading through me like fucking sunshine. I want to bask in it, to claim it for my own.

We've heard rumors for a while that Cillian had a niece hidden away somewhere in the city, but we were never able to confirm. I guess now we know. She's here, right in front of me, glowing like the sun, even in her sleep.

Tempting me, even in repose.

I should shimmy back down the tree and return another night, but I don't. I can't. She compels me toward her, beckoning like a siren. I slip through the window like a shadow, landing on silent feet beside the bed. I crouch at her side, watching.

I tell myself that's all I intend to do. Watch her. But even before I see the rope marks on her wrist, I know I'm a liar. I know I don't intend to leave here without her. But as soon as I see those, cold rage washes through me and everything that came before ceases to matter. That motherfucker has been tying her to her bed.

That ends here and now.

I have no right to take this girl from her bed. What happens to her isn't my business. But the monster inside me...the one that lives on blood and pain and the fucking misery I cause motherfuckers like her uncle? He disagrees. I'll take her just because I can. Just to remind her uncle that there are bigger monsters in this city than he could ever hope to be.

And this one just chose his queen.

She will be mine. Body and soul. I won't stop until she is. Whatever I have to do, no matter what it takes, this girl will belong to me.

I've broken every law there is to break. I've lied, cheated, robbed, and killed. I've never taken a woman against her will. I've never taken one to my bed at all, in fact. But this one leaves here with me tonight.

It isn't what I came here for, but it's how this night ends.

And when she wakes in my bed?

Well, she'll learn what it means to belong to me then. But hell itself won't stop me from taking her from this place.

Rafe won't like it. In fact, he'll be furious. Taking Cillian's niece? How many times have we made the same fucking mistake lately, and it's almost cost us everything? I know better. I just don't care.

This has nothing to do with Rafe, my oath, or *La Cosa Nostra*. This exists outside of *La Cosa Nostra*. This is bigger than my debt to Rafe. This is about Cillian and teaching him how the fuck to treat the women in his care. I've known men like him. One raised me. And because of him, my mother is dead. So is the woman who loved me when she couldn't. And I spent a lifetime searching for the sister she gave up because my father left her with nothing.

Men like them don't deserve to keep breathing. And men like me relish in punishing them for every fucking sin.

I drag myself away from the girl's bed long enough to slip downstairs to do what I came to do. When I step outside her room, my blood boils. The rest of the house is dead silent. Cillian doesn't even have a guard posted to keep watch. He's too arrogant, too confident in his safety here in his home. He's a fool.

Tonight, he'll pay for his arrogance when I take his niece from beneath his nose.

I hide the listening devices throughout the house, moving quickly and soundlessly from one room to the other. If anyone finds the devices, they won't trace them back to us. They'll assume it's the FBI, or the DEA, or the ATF, or Chicago PD, or any number of other law enforcement agencies who make life difficult for men like us.

Once the devices are planted, I unlock the front door and then circle back to the kitchen. I grab the mask I found on the table there, stuffing it into my pocket. And then I slip back upstairs.

Within minutes, I'm back in Cillian's niece's bedroom, and no one in the house has a fucking clue I'm even there. The prick deserves to lose her if this is how well he guards her. There's a monster roaming his halls, preparing to snatch his niece from her goddamn bed, and he's asleep down the hall, oblivious.

Would he stop me if he knew? I don't know, and I want to kill him for that realization alone. My hands ache to reach for my knives to slit his miserable throat. But I ignore the desire for now and don the mask I stole from him, pulling it down over my face.

I grab a bag from the closet and pack a few things into it for her so she'll have clothes. I won't leave her to run around in her little nightshirt and panties. At least not while we're on the move.

Once I have a few things, I drape the bag over my arm and make my way back to the bed. I scoop her up, blanket and all. She stirs in my arms, snuggling up against my chest with a little puff of sound that goes straight to my cock.

Does she even realize what's happening to her right now?

No, of course she doesn't. She'd be screaming in terror if she did, not cuddling up against me like she's safe as houses. She is, though. She might not know it or believe it. When she wakes, I doubt she'll trust a fucking word I have to say. But one thing she'll always be with me is safe.

I don't want to hurt her. I'll kill anyone who tries. I just want to fuck my way into her soul and conquer every single inch of it. It will be mine. No matter how long it takes, I'll lay claim to her body and soul.

I wait until I'm out of the city before I call Mattia on a secure line.

"Domani," he says, not asking questions. He rarely does. We know enough not to trust even the most secure lines we've got. The fucking feds are always listening, always watching. Especially since Athena White left the fold and married Diego last year.

Losing one of their own agents to the mafia? It was a bitter pill to swallow for them, I'm sure.

I hope they're choking on it.

"I'm heading out for a few days," I say casually. "But I dropped off the mail on my way out." In other words, the devices are where they need to be, and I'm getting the fuck out of Dodge.

"Good to know," he says. "I'll look through it." He pauses. "Did you see our new friend on your way out?"

"I didn't see anyone," I lie, glancing toward the woman sleeping in the passenger seat beside me. She still hasn't stirred. Did Cillian drug her? Possibly.

I don't know how to explain her presence or what I did. Mattia knows how I amuse myself, but it's not something we've ever discussed openly. There's never been a need. The men I've killed deserved to die. That's all Mattia ever needed to know.

Tonight is an anomaly. I didn't kill Cillian. I kidnapped the niece he hurt. And that's not a conversation to be had over the phone.

It's not one I'm willing to have while she's in the city, either.

If I wasn't careful enough, it'll be a matter of hours before Cillian knows that I'm the one who took her from right underneath his nose. He knows who I am and who I work for. He'll know exactly where to go looking for her.

And Mattia will have to choose between turning us over or going to war. I'm fully aware of the risk I took.

But if I'm not in the city, it'll buy us a little time. I'm going to need it because I'm not giving her back to her uncle. Not for Mattia. Not for Rafe. Not for anyone. She has rope burns on her wrists. If I have to kill everyone in her family to keep her out of their hands, so be it.

And if I have to fight my own? It's not something I relish doing. I've always been ten toes down for my family. I've always kept my vows, even when doing so turned friend to foe and drew lines in the sand that not even time erased. But I'm not giving her back.

"You heading to Texas?" Mattia asks.

"Nah. Scarlett just had a baby. She doesn't need me in her hair. I'm heading to my place in Rockford," I say. It's not a lie. That is where I'm currently headed. I have no intention of staying there for long. But I don't want him sending anyone to Silver Spoon Falls looking for me. The sister I spent my entire life looking for and her family are there. The last thing I want is for this shit to spill over into her life when I promised her husband, Finn, that it never would.

She has an entire MC and the Arakas family looking out for her, not to mention the man I've got in town protecting her from afar, but I still intend to keep my shit as far from her as possible. This isn't her life, and it shouldn't have to be. She's happy and thriving exactly where she is.

This shit? The constant bullshit and fuckery? She wasn't made for it. She's soft, sweet, innocent. I want to keep her that way.

I owe that much to Silvia, her mother. She was my nanny.

"Enjoy," Mattia says. "I'll call you soon."

"Later," I disconnect, fully aware that this might be the last time we talk as equals in the family. I made my bed, though. I'm not afraid to lie in it.

Chapter Two

Finley

As soon as I come awake, I know something is different. My eyes aren't even open, and I feel the change in the air. It isn't as heavy as usual, crushing my lungs as if each breath has invisible weights tied to it...or as if the air has grown dangerously thin.

There's something else in the air, too. A masculine spice I've never smelled before. It's not my uncle's cologne. I don't recognize it from one of my cousins either. It's an intoxicating scent, one that makes my stomach flutter. I keep my eyes closed as I take a deep breath, pulling it deeper into my lungs.

"You're awake."

My eyes pop open as the rumbling growl washes over me.

The deepest hazel eyes I've ever seen connect with mine across the room. For a minute, everything else falls out of focus. All I see is the gorgeous giant leaning against the wall, his sleeves rolled up, his eyes locked on me. He's so beautiful in a fierce, warriorlike kind of way. Everything about him is dark. His hair, his eyes, the stubble on his jaw. Even the look in his eyes, as if he was born of darkness.

He isn't one of my uncle's men. I don't know who he is.

And we aren't in my room. I don't know where we are.

But in this moment, when I should probably feel overwhelming panic and fear, the first emotion that hits me is relief. It's an illogical, unreasonable response. But I've spent my entire life in a cage of glass, surrounded by monsters.

If this man is one, too, at least I'm not in that damn house any longer. At least I'll die staring at something other than the pretty gilding my uncle surrounded me with.

I'd rather die free than live another day in hell.

"My name is Domani Brambilla. I took you from your uncle's compound a few hours ago."

Domani Brambilla. The name is familiar. I've heard my uncle and cousins speak it before. But I still don't know this man. I know one thing, though. He's every bit as dangerous as they are. Moreso, perhaps. Because when they speak his name, they speak it in whispers, as if afraid of what saying it too loudly will conjure. He's the bogeyman to my uncle.

And I guess the bogeyman exists after all. He's standing in front of me, isn't he?

"Are you going to kill me?" I ask, far more calmly than I feel. My heart thumps against my breastbone in jarring thuds, each hard enough to rattle my bones. I don't know if it's fear or if it's the fact that he hasn't taken his eyes off me, though. He's just staring at me, a hunger in his gaze that has the same response fighting to rise to the surface within me.

How long has it been since I've felt anything but cold, simmering rage and hopeless despair? I can't remember. Cillian has kept me locked in that damn house since he moved me to Chicago almost two years ago. I'm twenty-one years old, and I'm a prisoner. My life is not my own. It never has been. Like I said, I've been surrounded by monsters.

Except they smile in my face and call themselves my family. And just when I think they mean it, they lock me in my room or tie me to the bed to keep me there. I'm a prisoner in my own life, held hostage by the men my father trusted to guard me with their lives. Their insidiousness is perverse, and they love every minute of my torment.

"No," Domani says, growling the word as if he's speaking a vow. "No one is going to kill you, *mio sole*."

"Then why..." I pause and lick my lips. His gaze follows the path of my tongue. "Why did you take me?"

"You don't belong in that place," he says as if that explains everything. It doesn't. Not even close. "What's your name?"

Should I lie to him? Probably. Do I? No.

"Finley Brennan."

"Finley," he repeats, rolling it around on his tongue. It sounds sinful on his lips. Like a kiss and a seductive promise. "I'm not going to hurt you, Finley. But I'm not going to let you go, either. You belong to me now."

There it is. The fire. The anger. A normal response to waking up in a stranger's bed after falling asleep in my own. Delayed, perhaps. But I'm not broken, after all. Anger rushes through me, filling me like a balloon.

"I belong to no one, Domani," I say, defiant. He may have kidnapped me, but that doesn't give him ownership over me. My uncle may be a lot of things, but he didn't raise a coward. I won't play along with this man or bow to him just because he says I should.

I may have spent most of my life locked away, but one thing my family has never been able to take from me was my own free will. I won't give it up for this man, either. I belong to no one. My soul is my own.

For some reason, my response amuses him. His lips quirk into a simile of a grin. He's a beautiful monster, hauntingly so. The darkness in his gaze is captivating. What has he seen and done that keeps him awake at night? Whatever it is, he wears it well, even if it eats at him.

"No?" He pushes away from the wall, stepping toward the bed. I refuse to flinch away, refuse to tremble in fear, or let this man think he scares me. My family may be afraid of him, but I won't be. I refuse. "Your soul was mine the second I stepped into your bedroom and saw you in your bed, Finley. If your uncle wanted to keep you, he never should have let a motherfucker like me get close to you." He crouches beside the bed, reaching toward me.

I lock my muscles, refusing to flinch or cower. Refusing to show fear.

His palm brushes over my right breast, and then he rolls my nipple between his thumb and forefinger, his eyes locked on the sight. I shiver, my teeth clamped together to keep myself from moaning out loud. I shouldn't like the way it feels. I should *hate* the feel of his hands on me and the way he looks at me.

I don't. I hate that I don't hate it. Something in me responds to him, woman to man. It likes the feel of his hand on my body and the way he looks at me as if he can't stop himself. It likes the fact that he took me from that damnable place without permission and thinks he can own me.

I'm my own worst enemy. I know this. It's exactly why my uncle got away with keeping me locked away for so long. I should have been his worst nightmare. Instead, I was my own. I smiled and played along, letting them think I believed they were doing what they did for my own good, and every day, another piece of my soul died. And the whole time, I said nothing. I just smiled.

I knew what they were capable of doing. I witnessed them doing it over and over again. To other women. To the men they killed. They had no remorse. They have no souls. I did what I had to do to survive. But my soul? Well, I sacrificed more than my pride along the way.

Now, this man has me, he's touching me...and I should be fighting like hell. Instead, I'm reveling in the first human touch I've felt in years. It's fucked up. And I love it.

What's that they say about broken people? Oh, right. They can't be put back together again. No matter how much glue you use, the cracks and crevices remain. I guess that's me now. Broken beyond repair.

At least I'm in good company. Because if anyone understands what that's like, I think it might be this man.

"You will be mine in every way, *mio sole*. You can fight it. You can hate me. In the end, the pieces will align the same way." His gaze flits across my face. "You'll have my ring on your finger, and I'll kill anyone who even thinks about trying to take you."

"My uncle? My cousins?"

"Anyone," he snarls.

"Good," I whisper, arching into his touch. "I hope you make it hurt."

Deadly malice flares in his eyes before they turn to stone. He pinches my nipple again and then slowly pulls his hand away. "What did they do to you, Finley?"

I sit up slowly. Only then do I realize I'm still in the same crop top and panties I wore to bed last night. The purple blanket from my bed is draped over a chaise across the room, but the rest of the room is black. Black sheets, black comforter, black furniture. It's expensive and elegant. And as unrelentingly dark as this man's soul.

We're in his home. I'm not sure why I'm so certain, but I just am. It matches him.

I consider pulling the covers up over myself to hide my body from his gaze, but then say screw it. He's already seen everything. He's had his hand on my breast. I'm not going to cower and hide. I'm not going to crumble and fall apart. I've never been the delicate girl who cries at the drop of a hat. This is a big hat and a monumental drop, but I won't cry now, either. So I'm half naked in a stranger's bed. It's not even the strangest part of my night.

"Tell me," he growls, rising to his feet.

"I'll answer your questions if you answer mine," I negotiate. It's the one thing my uncle taught me...find a place of power and do whatever it takes to keep it. That's how I grew up. That's the big lesson I learned in life. Knowledge is power. Right now, I have neither.

He seems amused again, as if he knows exactly what I'm doing. But he plays along. "Fine. You ask your question. I'll ask mine, *mio sole*."

"Why were you at my uncle's house?"

"To plant listening devices."

"Why?"

"That's two questions, Finley."

"No, it's one. You just gave an incomplete response to the first."

The smile he gives this time is no simile. It's genuine. "Fair enough. Your uncle is a problem for us. This city belongs to *La Cosa Nostra*. He's forgotten that. We're handling the problem."

"By planting listening devices."

"Yes."

"Ho–"

"That's another question," he says, cutting me off. "It's my turn. What did they do to you?"

"Nothing." It's not entirely untrue. It's not necessarily the truth, either. It's the word that dances that razor's edge in between reality and fiction. The one that says nothing and everything all at once.

"And yet you don't care if I kill them."

"Monsters are monsters, Domani."

He plants a knee on the bed, his face suddenly looming in front of mine like a snake striking. One hand curls around my jaw, gently tipping my head back. The anger banked in his eyes turns my nipples to glass points. "Don't lie to me, Finley. What did they do to you?"

"Nothing," I whisper, my heart pounding an erratic beat. "They didn't do anything to me, Domani."

"And yet you have rope burns on your wrists and hatred in your eyes."

"Do you know how many people women they hurt in that house? How many people they killed?" I ask, licking my lips. His face is inches from mine, so close I see the gold flecks in his eyes. I smell the mint of his toothpaste on his breath. I want him to kiss me, as crazy as it is. He loathes my uncle, and so do I. He's the lesser of two evils. The enemy of my enemy and all. But I'd be lying if I said that's all the desire was. It's not. I know that on a fundamental level.

There's something about this man that tempts me even though it shouldn't. There's something about him I crave even though I shouldn't. He wants to own me...and part of me wants to let him.

"Do you know how many people I heard begging for their lives, Domani? How many times I laid in bed while the stench of burning flesh filled the house from the in-cinerator in the basement?"

"*Cristo*. You were there?"

"One year, nine months, eighteen days."

"What are you counting, *mio sole*?"

"How long it's been since I arrived in Chicago." I swallow. "How long it's been since I left that house."

Shock widens his eyes, followed by fury. "You've been locked in that fucking house for over a year?"

"Welcome to life as an Irish *banphrionsa*. I envy your *principessas*. At least they have freedom. I don't. I never have," I say quietly. "Since the day my father was murdered and Cillian took over as head of our family, I've been a prisoner in my own life, trapped like a rat in a cage."

"How old were you?"

"Eleven."

"How long has he been tying you to your bed?"

"On and off for years. Every time he decides I'm thinking about running away." I snort indelicately. "As if I could ever escape him."

"You've escaped him now, Finley."

For the moment, at least. But freedom comes with a price. And the one I suspect this man wants me to pay might be higher than I can afford. But I don't tell him that.

"How are listening devices supposed to handle my uncle for the Italian mafia?" I ask instead.

"He's dirty," he says, his hand still around my throat. I don't really mind. It's kind of...nice, actually.

He's comforting to me, like the smell of aged whiskey and cigars. My father's office always smelled of both. I used to curl up under his desk and read until I passed out, completely content in the knowledge that I was safe. I feel that way now. It's madness, of course. This man just kidnapped me. He wants to own me. But he tells me I'm safe, and every fiber of my being believes him.

Like I said, I'm my own worst enemy.

"We can't kill him without starting a war. We intend to let his people take out the trash for us."

I laugh abruptly. "You're a fool if you think they'll do your dirty work for you, Domani. You think they don't know that he's a snake? They've always known. Cillian and his family come before anyone and anything else to him. He'll always put himself and his sons above everything else, including his oaths. They knew this when they sent him here. They sent him anyway."

"Why?"

"Why did you take me?"

"Because you're mine," he growls. "Why did they send him here?"

"Because they wanted a piece of Chicago, and he was the only one with the power to pry it from the Valentino family's grip. If you think they care that he's skimming from the top, you're wrong. If you think they care that he's doing deals behind their backs, you're wrong. He's exactly where they want him." I eye him sideways. "And even if they did take him out, Cian is every bit as vicious and ambitious as he is. He'd take his place and bring war to your doorstep anyway."

"Cian is his son?"

"His oldest, yes. Why did you take me?" It's the only answer I really want. Why did he take me? Why did he pluck me from my bed in the dead of night and bring me here? My mind won't rest until I have an answer...a *real* answer, something tangible I can understand.

"Because you belong to me," he says again. "How many people work for him?"

"Hundreds? Thousands? I don't know. I wasn't a trusted confidant, Domani. I was a pretty little bird in a glass cage who heard things she wasn't supposed to hear. Why did you take me?"

"Because you were the only fucking thing I saw when I climbed through your window," he growls, his hand tightening on my throat. He doesn't cut off my air supply. He holds me captive, pinning me in place with his intensity more than his hand. "Because I saw you, and I knew I'd go to fucking war to keep you. You're mine, *mio sole*." His lips brush mine, his kiss hard and unyielding but somehow full of fervent devotion, too, as if he's staking a claim and making a vow at the same time. "*Mine*."

His words rip through me. I feel them striking chords in my soul, each note shaking loose a profound sense of belonging that makes me ache. For the first time since I woke up in his room and heard his voice, I know terror.

This man will be my savior or my destruction. He'll lead me to heaven...or send me straight to hell. I don't know which it will be. And I'm petrified of how much I ache to find out.

Chapter Three

Domani

"You should get dressed," I say, dragging myself away from Finley before I do something I know I'll live long enough to regret. I'm burning for her, the fires growing hotter every minute I spend touching any part of her perfect body. It's exquisite torture.

Forcing her to hand over what I want isn't an option. Her willing submission is part of what I crave. I want her to yield. I want her to cede her soul, handing it over to me without reservation. Only then will I take what I want.

But I won't play fair along the way. If her uncle taught her survival, this is what my father taught me. He was an unscrupulous bastard, rotten to the core. He lied, cheated, and manipulated his way into beds all across this city. And when that didn't work, he simply took what he wanted. I'll never do that. But seducing this girl? That I will do. With a fucking smile on my face.

"I won't be your obedient little toy, Domani," she says, watching me as if she's trying to figure me out. As if she knows exactly what I'm thinking. "You can send me back to my uncle or kill me. I don't care. But I won't be your little plaything."

"Who says I want a toy, Finley?" I ask, scooping her bag from the floor. "I already told you what I want. My ring. Your finger." I place the bag on the bed beside her. "Get dressed. We're leaving in ten minutes."

"Leaving?" She gapes up at me. "Where are we going?"

"For now? My cabin," I say. "After that? We'll see."

The allure of the road is a powerful temptation for one who hasn't seen anything but her own prison for so long. She bounds off the bed, almost desperately eager. It's as fucking sad as it is cute. She's been locked up for nearly two years, trapped and listening to every vile thing they've done inside that house.

When I get my hands on Cillian, I may kill him for that alone.

Her hands hover over her bag. She turns her head, seeking me out over her shoulder. "This is from my closet."

"It is."

"You packed a bag for me?"

"Figured you'd need some things." I shrug like it's not a big deal. Evidently, it is to her, though. She looks like she wants to cry.

"Thank you," she whispers.

"Get dressed." I nod toward the door across the room. "The bathroom is right there."

She scoops the bag up and flees toward the bathroom, her gorgeous ass swaying with every step. I watch the entire time, unable to take my eyes off of her. One day soon, I'm going to know exactly what that ass feels like wrapped around my cock.

One day very soon.

She slips inside the bathroom, closing the door.

I stride toward the closet to grab a few things I need. Guns, ammo, and a few more knives. You know, basic shit. I load it all into a duffle bag, open the safe, and pull out two stacks of cash. I add most to the bag and then stuff several thousand dollars in my wallet. I also roll a few more bills and put them in my sock. If we have to run, we'll have to ditch the car, my cards, everything. I need enough cash to make sure we can make it to my safehouse in Washington.

Once that's done, I toss clothes on top and zip the bag. When I turn around, Finley's standing outside the closet, watching me. She changed into a green sweater and skinny jeans that mold to her legs, making them seem miles long. I chose well because she looks fucking perfect.

"That's a lot of cash," she says quietly.

"Just a precaution."

"And the guns?"

"Also a precaution." I hook the bag over my shoulder, muttering a curse when the guns jostle together, making her scowl. "Are you ready?"

"You expect my uncle to come after me, don't you?"

"We'll talk about it on the way." I hold out my hand for her bag.

She reluctantly hands over the bag and then follows me out of the room. We don't speak as we make our way through the condo and out to the garage. She stops in her tracks when she sees the small incinerator in the corner.

"I don't burn bodies in it, *mio sole*," I murmur.

"But you burn something in it."

"Yes."

She shivers, wrapping her arms around herself.

"Come on." I hit the button on the keyfob, unlocking the doors to the Range Rover. Her brows rise, but she doesn't say anything as I help her into the passenger seat. Once she's settled, I put our bags in the back seat and then grab some shit from the shelves—blankets, flashlights, an emergency kit with food, water, and medical supplies.

I've been in the mafia for a long fucking time. If you're going to run, you better be prepared. There is no stopping once you start. I know the drill. If it comes to that...shit, I hope it doesn't come to that. But if it does, we'll be ready.

I load everything into the SUV, slam the door, and then climb in beside Finley.

She spends the first part of the drive gaping at the city around us. Rockford isn't nearly as large or as bustling as Chicago, but it has its own charm. Historic Victorian homes and buildings mingle with those built more recently, all nestled between scenic landscapes and forest preserves. For one who hasn't seen anything but a rundown mansion and her own family for almost two years, it's probably close to magical, especially in the early morning light.

We're a few miles out of town, the sun cresting the horizon, before she speaks.

"What do you burn in the incinerator?"

"My clothes."

"Why?"

"You know why, Finley," I say gently, not willing to lie to her about who I am and what I do. I won't pretend I'm something I'm not. She deserves honesty, at the very minimum.

She exhales a shuddering breath. "You kill people too."

I wish I could tell her no, but I can't. I lost count of the people I killed a long time ago. Their faces stopped haunting me over a decade ago. I am who I am. I've done what I've done. I can't take it back. I wouldn't even if I could. The sins I committed saved the lives of the people who matter. If that damns me to hell, I'll stand with my head held high on Judgment Day and accept my fate.

"I have," I say. "Most of them knew what awaited them when they made the choices they made."

"That doesn't justify murder, Domani."

"I'm not trying to justify it, *mio sole*. I merely explain. If you're looking for a reason to view me as anything other than a monster, I don't have one for you. I've committed damn near every crime there is to commit. I know what I am. I know what I do. I don't justify it, Finley. But if you're looking for a reason to condemn me, let it be the truth. The men I killed knew what was coming for them. Some deserved it far more than others, but none were innocent. None were victims. In this life, it's kill or be killed. I chose not to be killed or to allow the same fate to befall the people who matter."

"The people who matter? You mean the Valentino family."

"Sometimes, yes. But not always. Sometimes, the people I protected had nothing to do with the Valentino family or the mafia." I cut my eyes in her direction. "Sometimes, they were like you, just trying to survive men like your uncle. He isn't the only monster I've met. He's not even the worst."

She processes this for a long moment and then nods. She doesn't have to ask what I mean. She knows. Finley is smart, far too smart for her own good, I think. "Did you take those girls too?"

"No. I took care of their problems and walked away. They never even knew I existed."

"But you took me," she whispers.

"I told you; you belong to me."

She rolls her head to the side to look at me. "Did you ever think maybe you're just crazy, Domani?"

I chuckle at her question. "The thought crossed my mind a time or two, *mio sole*. But no, this isn't madness. It's something else. Something bigger." I glance at her again to see her eyes locked on my face as if she's really trying to understand me. "I know you feel it, too."

She swallows, shifting her gaze away from me. But not before I see the acknowledgment in her eyes. She does feel it. The electric charge between us. The irrevocable certainty that this is where she's supposed to be. Even before I saw the rope burn on her wrist, I knew she was leaving that house with me. If that makes me a fucking monster, I'll own it.

We fall silent again. It's not uncomfortable or awkward. It's just...silent. Still. Peaceful, even. I feel her gaze on me periodically as the SUV flies down the road, quickly putting distance between us and the mess I'm leaving behind. But mostly, she looks out the window, avidly curious as only one starved for sight is.

"You told me that we'd talk about my uncle in the car," she finally says. "You expect him to come after me, don't you?"

"Don't you?" I ask instead of answering.

Her slumped shoulders are answer enough. She knows he'll come after her. "I don't think he cares about me. I could die tomorrow, and he wouldn't shed a tear. But he hates losing. You took me from his home. He'll be angry about that." She pauses. "And I'm valuable to him."

"Why?"

"Because he wants to keep control of my trust fund. He's the executor. He has final say over the trust fund until I'm twenty-five unless I get married or file to have him removed." She grimaces. "I think he plans to cling to control for as long as possible."

"Why? He has his own money."

"He has my dad's money," she snorts. "Everything he owns, he got from my dad. And it's a drop in the bucket compared to what's in that trust fund, Domani."

"*Cristo.* What happens when you turn twenty-five? What's his plan?"

She shrugs one shoulder. "Kill me? Marry me off to one of his cronies? I don't know, but I'm sure there is a plan. There always is with him."

There's no question then. He will be coming after her with everything he's got. And he'll go to war to get her back.

Cazzo. I fucking knew my night was going to end in a bunch of bullshit as soon as Mattia popped in to see me. I didn't kill anyone, and I'm not bleeding either, but somehow, I'm more fucked than ever before.

But it changes nothing. Actually, it changes everything. Because it's more important than ever that Cillian not get his hands on her. Rafe and Mattia may disagree when the stakes are this high. She's Irish, not Italian. We stay out of their shit, and they stay out of ours. That's how it's supposed to work. But I won't condemn an innocent woman to a life under Cillian's rule. I won't send one to her death. Especially not this woman.

He'll kill her or marry her off to get her money. And considering the fact that he ties her to the goddamn bed, I'm not willing to gamble on him marrying her off. Even if she didn't belong to me, it's not a risk I'd take.

I have to kill her uncle. And hope like hell that her cousin is willing to negotiate once the motherfucker is dead. If not...we're going to war. And it's going to end with my head on a pike.

Rafe will put it there himself.

Chapter Four

Finley

"Wake up, *mio sole*." Domani runs the back of his hand down my cheek, speaking softly. I fight the urge to nuzzle into his touch, even though it's precisely what I want to do. We've been in the car for hours, nothing but the hum of the road to keep us company. Every time I breathe, his scent fills my lungs.

It's lulling me toward something vast and deep. Or maybe that's complacency talking. I'm not sure. But the longer I spend with him, the more I soften toward him. I know who he is and what he's about, and it doesn't frighten me nearly as much as it should.

"I'm not asleep."

"Little liar," Domani chuckles. "You've been sleeping for the last hour."

"I've been resting my eyes."

He chuckles again, the rich, decadent sound hitting me deep in my stomach. He has an incredible laugh. Who am I kidding? If ever a man was made for sin, it's this one. Everything about him is decadent and sensual. "You missed the last of the drive while you were resting them, *mio sole*. We're here."

I pop my eyes open and glance around. We're in the middle of the forest, massive trees shooting up into the sky all around us. It's beautiful, but there's nothing out here. "We're here? Where?"

Another simile of a grin touches his lips. "We have to walk from here, Finley."

The thought of walking through the forest excites me. It's been...a long dang time since I was outside, free to roam. I can't even remember the last time I had fresh air and open space. But I peer through the trees anyway, anxious.

"Is it safe?" I ask, hating how small and vulnerable I sound.

He runs the back of his hand down my cheek again. "Perfectly, *tesoro*. Anything out there will be more afraid of us than we are of it."

"No." I shake my head. "You don't understand. I mean, is it safe to leave the car? What if we have to leave in a hurry?"

"Ah," he says, understanding. "This is the back of the property, Finley. I'm leaving the car here for that very reason. There is another at the cabin and a small gravel road leading to it. We're going in this way."

"Another precaution," I mumble.

"Precisely."

"You take a lot of those, don't you?" I shift my gaze back to him, infinitely curious about this man and the life he's lived. I know the things he's done. But how many have come back to haunt him? Not his mind, but his reality? Do his demons chase him in the waking world, or do they only rear their heads at night? He knows so much about me and my life, but I have more questions than answers about him and his. We aren't on equal footing, and I don't like it.

"I do. They keep me alive. Now, they'll keep you safe."

I take his word for it and unlatch my seatbelt. He climbs from the SUV and circles around, grabbing our bags from the back before he offers his hand to me. I take it, letting him help me out. I expect him to release it once I'm on my feet, but he doesn't. He tugs me toward his massive body, getting in my personal space again.

I tip my head back to look up at him.

"You said my name in your sleep," he murmurs, staring down at me as if I'm a puzzle he desperately wishes to solve.

"Did I? How strange," I say, pretending I have no idea why I'd do that. I know, though. I remember exactly what I was dreaming about, but hell itself couldn't pry the truth from my lips. Some secrets are too delicious to share.

Another of those almost smiles graces his full lips. He lifts my hand, brushing a kiss across my knuckles. "Keep your secrets for now, *mio sole*. But you'll tell me by the time the sun sets tonight."

"No, I won't."

"You will, but keep telling yourself that, Finley." He releases my hand, slamming the door to the Rover. "Come on. We need to get moving."

I stare after him for a moment, surprised that he just walks away and leaves me standing there. Either he isn't worried that I'll run, or he doesn't care if I do. Do I even want to run? Freedom is right there. All I have to do is turn and go in the opposite direction, and it's mine. For the first time in my life, I'll be on my own. No one telling me what to do. No one holding me against my will. No one in charge of me but myself.

It's a powerful temptation. Overwhelmingly so. But even if I walk away, I'm not free. It'll just be an illusion. The threat of my uncle still hangs over my head like a sword. He's the specter haunting my future. That doesn't change just because I'm out in the world on my own.

I need Domani. He's my one shot at true freedom, and he knows I know it. That's why he isn't afraid I'll run. I need him. I need the man he is and the things he's done. I need his brutal savagery, and the blood on his hands. If I'm ever going to be free of my uncle...I need this man to kill him.

I guess if he's a monster, so am I.

I start walking after him. He pauses a few feet ahead and waits for me to catch up.

"You didn't run," he says when I make it to his side.

"To where? It's not like I have anywhere else to go."

Domani grunts but doesn't say anything.

We walk in silence for several moments. The forest is still, but it isn't quiet. Small sounds echo around us. The rustling of wind through the leaves. The chatter of birds. The chirp of instincts. There are a dozen different sounds, all making up a song I haven't heard in years. It's beautiful. I'd forgotten how much. But it isn't soothing.

My soul is scraped raw; my wounds laid bare.

"So long as he's alive, I'll never be free, Domani," I whisper.

"His life was over the moment I saw the rope burn on your wrist, *mio sole*." He tips his head down to look at me, his eyes hard and dark. Malevolent. "He'll pay in blood for what he's done, this I promise."

I slip my hand into his, hopeful and sad at the same time. I loved my uncle once upon a time. He was my hero after my dad died. But the thing about heroes? Eventually, you realize they're all too human, invariably possessed of the same faults, flaws, and foibles as the rest of us. My uncle's faults are many and massive. He isn't a good man. He never was. He was just good at pretending.

A few minutes later, the cabin comes into view ahead, nestled in the dead center of a clearing. The trees just stop suddenly on all sides, leaving the cabin completely exposed. A creek cuts through the property on the far side, but the rest is grassy. The single-story log cabin itself is charming and adorable, like a little fairytale cottage plucked for a storybook. An attached garage is situated to the left. It's not at all something I would have associated with Domani Brambilla.

"This is yours?" I ask, craning my head back to look up at him.

"It is."

"Wow."

"You like it?"

"I love it," I whisper, hurrying my steps.

Domani halts me. "Slow, *mio sole*. I want to make sure everything is all right first."

I stop walking to look up at him. He's staring at the cabin, but he seems tense, more than he has all day. He likes his precautions, but I don't think this is one of those. It's something else. Something happened while I was sleeping. "They know I'm missing, don't they?"

"They do," he says without looking at me.

"Do they know you took me?"

The fact that he doesn't answer me is answer enough.

"I'm going to throw up," I whisper, crouching beside a tree as a wave of nausea climbs up my throat. I fight it back, refusing to vomit in front of this man. Refusing to panic over this. So they know I'm missing and I'm with Domani. They were going to find out sooner or later. It was inevitable.

"Breathe, Finley," Domani says, crouching at my side. "You're okay. Just breathe, *tesoro*."

I inhale a lungful of air and promptly choke on it.

Domani curses, dragging me into his arms. I shouldn't, but I burrow into him, pressing my face to his throat as tremors wrack my body. I don't want to go back to hell. For the first time in a long time, I feel hope. I'm not ready to lose it. I don't think I'll survive losing it.

If I have to go back there...I'm going to my death.

Uncle Cillian will kill me for running. It'll be my pleas for mercy slipping through cracks in the doors. I'll be the next one to die in that house. And it'll be my burning flesh permeating every inch of space inside.

"You're safe," Domani whispers in my ear, holding me as if he doesn't plan on ever letting me go. "You're right here with me, and you're safe."

I want to believe him. God, I want it so fucking badly. But one thing I've never been? Naïve. I'm not safe, and neither is he. Right now, we're the furthest thing from it.

"How are you feeling?" Domani asks an hour later, watching me carefully from across the kitchen table. His powerful arms cross his broad chest, pulling his suit jacket tight across his shoulders.

"Good. Better," I whisper, pushing food around on my plate. He stopped at a grocery store while I slept and bought supplies. As soon as we got here, he made me lunch. I didn't eat much, but it helped. I feel calmer, less like I might crack apart at the seams at any moment.

"Are you ready to talk?"

I shake my head, wanting to forestall the conversation for as long as possible. I know it's a childish move. Not talking about the situation won't change it. It won't make us any safer or reshape our reality. But this is the first time in almost two years that I haven't been under my uncle's thumb.

If I'm going to be dragged back there or killed or be forced to spend the rest of my life running or whatever the case may be, I want to spend at least one day pretending that I'm not choking on the taste of freedom.

Is that too much to ask?

"No?" Domani asks, one brow raised.

"I don't want to talk about it. I don't want to think about it. For today, I just want to be a normal girl," I say, setting my fork on my plate. "I want to enjoy the fact that I'm not trapped in that house, slowly losing my mind. Can I do that for one day, Domani? Please?"

He doesn't say anything, clearly hesitant to let me deny reality when reality might come crashing down on us at any moment.

"Please?" I plead, willing to beg if that's what it takes. "I know it's stupid. But Cillian has controlled every moment of my life since I was eleven. For ten years, I've been under his rule. Tomorrow, I'll deal with the fact that I'm still not out from underneath him. I'll go back to living in the real world where my life is infinitely complicated, and the only way it gets better is by having the man who kidnapped me kill the man who raised me. But right now, I need five minutes to breathe."

"I didn't kidnap you, Finley."

I narrow my eyes on him. "That's your takeaway from my plea for mercy? That you didn't kidnap me?"

"It seemed relevant." He cracks a smile so I launch a piece of bread at him like a missile. The man has ninja-like reflexes. I miss by a mile, but he snaps his arm out, plucking the bread from midair as it sails past his head. He doesn't even look at it. He just freaking grabs it and sets it beside his plate. His eyes meet mine, his gaze heated. "If you're going to throw shit at me, don't miss, Finley."

"Oops. Slipped," I lie, batting my lashes at him. He doesn't intimidate me. I'm not afraid of him. Maybe I should be. Hell, I know I should be. But I'm not. There are bigger monsters waiting for me in the dark than the one who carried me out of my cage.

He watches me for a long moment, his gaze shooting off sparks. He isn't mad, though. He's turned on. Lust swirls like clouds through his eyes. The only thing keeping him in his chair and off me is his own code of conduct, whatever ethos he ascribes to. Morality isn't a fixed absolute in his world. It's ever-changing. But I think if there is one thing that he stands firm on, it's this: he won't take what I don't offer him of my own free will.

He wants my soul. And he wants me to hand it to me.

God help us both, but the longer I spend with him, the more I think I might do just that. Not because I must but because I can. Because I want to know what he feels like all over me.

If that's wrong, so be it. I'd rather die in his arms than live clinging to the innocence that's never served me. I know what my uncle intends to use it for. If he doesn't kill me outright for running, he'll sell my virginity to the highest bidder. I'm a commodity in his world, a piece to move around the board. That's all I've ever been.

With Domani, though? I see glimmers of a different future, and I ache to reach for it. It's utterly terrifying. It's far too soon. We have too much still ahead of us. And yet, I ache anyway.

Perhaps I am naïve, after all.

"I know you didn't kidnap me," I whisper, handing him the first piece of my soul. "You saved me."

"Don't give me too much credit, *mio sole*. Even before I saw the rope burn, I intended to leave that house with you." His eyes burn into me. "Call that what you will."

"Temptation."

"That's one word for it," he mutters, his gaze running over me. He's so hard to read. I see the desire in his eyes. See how much he appreciates looking at me. Sometimes, I even get a sense of what he feels in any given moment. But what he's thinking? The stuff below the surface? He keeps both carefully locked away in those hazel depths.

"Tell me something about you."

He blinks at me, caught off guard by the abrupt question. "What do you want to know, Finley?"

"Anything."

"I've been in the mafia since I was eighteen."

I grimace. "Anything but that."

Another simile of a smile. "That's my life, *tesoro*. It's what I know."

"Fine. Why did you decide you wanted to initiate?"

"My father." He pushes his plate away from him, leaning back in his chair.

"He was in the mafia?"

Domani nods. "I didn't initiate to follow in his footsteps. I initiated to ensure he died like the *pezzo di merda* he was."

"You killed him?" I'm the one caught off guard this time. He says it so casually, as if he's simply reporting the weather. It's hard to imagine that he's talking about his own father.

"No. But I'm the one who signed his death warrant," he says softly. "I turned over the evidence that ensured he didn't walk away from his crimes."

I don't get the sense he did it lightly. Whatever his reason, he had one. I want to ask, but I don't.

He tells me anyway.

"He deserved to rot," he growls, meeting my gaze. "My mother took her life because of him. My nanny spent hers searching for their daughter—my sister—because of him. Countless women still live in fear because of what he took from them."

"He's the reason...?" I trail off, unable to finish the question. He knows what I'm trying to ask, though.

"Yes."

I nod, satisfied with the answer. It's more truth than I expected from him today. I understand him and the kind of man he is more now than I did five minutes ago. He may think he's a monster—and perhaps he does monstrous things—but this monster has a heart. And it still bleeds because of the man who raised him. He still atones for sins that aren't his and never were.

No, he isn't a monster. He's what a monster creates. I guess I am, too.

"Come." He rises from the table, holding out his hand to me. "We'll pretend the world doesn't exist today, *mio sole*. And tomorrow, we'll go to war."

I don't hesitate to take his hand.

Chapter Five

Domani

"I'm not getting in there," Finley says, looking at me like I've lost my mind. Sunlight catches in her red hair, turning the strands to ropes of fiery copper. "It's probably freezing!"

"It's not." I crouch beside the small spring a short walk from the cabin, filling my hand with water and then lifting it toward her. "Feel for yourself."

She tips her head to the side, eyeing me hesitantly. And then she shrugs and skips forward, skimming her fingers through the water slowly running out of my hand. "It's hot," she says, surprised.

"It's fed by a hot spring underground. It stays this temperature year around."

"Even when it's freezing outside?"

"Even then," I confirm, rising to my feet. "You should soak. It's relaxing."

"You soak in this thing?"

"I have."

"You? Mr. Thousand Dollar Mafia Suit?"

My lips twitch at the doubt in her voice. Admittedly, I don't fit the mountain man persona. I belong out here about as well as a lion in the middle of a neighborhood park. But I've been shot, stabbed, and sliced all to hell. When I've needed to lie low, I've done it out here. And the spring helped soothe even the worst of my injuries.

That's not why I strip my jacket off. It's not why I pile my weapons on top of it, either. She watches me with wide eyes while I undo each button, slowly stripping my shirt from my body.

"You're getting in?" she asks, a breathless hue to her voice that makes my cock throb.

"Mmhmm." I yank my belt free, dropping it beside my clothes. I had no intention of going in until she got sassy with me. Now, wild horses couldn't keep me out of that fucking water. I kick my shoes off and drop my pants.

She cracks, dropping her gaze from my face. Her sharp intake of breath cracks *me* wide open. "Domani," she whispers, reaching out to me. Her fingers skim my side, running over a mass of scar tissue across my ribcage. "What happened to you?"

"The mafia happened, *tesoro*." I grab her hand, pulling her into me before she starts something I'm not nearly strong enough to stop. Her hands on my naked flesh are like brands, searing desire into every fiber of my being. I want her more than I've ever wanted anything.

Cristo. I ache. To possess. To consume. To wreck and ruin and destroy. And when it's over, to own. Not master to slave, authoritarian to subordinate, but two souls tied so tightly together they can't ever be undone. She can't exist without me, and I cease to exist without her. I want to own her and be owned by her in a way no one else ever can. There's some primal, instinctive hunger driving that need and *fuck*. It's overwhelming.

"There are so many of them. So many injuries. So much pain." Her voice trembles.

Is she crying for me?

I tip her head back to see the wet sheen of tears in her eyes. *Cristo*. She is weeping for me.

"Don't cry for me, *amorina*. I don't deserve your tears."

"You don't get to decide that, Domani. I do."

I curl my hand around her jaw, running my fingers beneath her eye. Her tears haven't fallen, but I imagine the feel of them on my fingertips anyway. No one has ever cried for me. I don't think anyone has ever found me worthy of tears. This girl shouldn't. I snatched her from her bed in the dark of night. And still, she weeps.

In this moment I decide two things. One, I'll never give her a reason to cry. And two, I'll be a man worthy of her tears.

I pull her flush against my body, slanting my mouth down over hers. I intend the kiss to be soft and sweet, a simple thank you. At least that's what I tell myself. But as soon as my lips touch hers, we ignite in a shower of sparks.

I don't even know which of us goes up first, but we burn together. I growl, plunging my hand into her hair to hold her still. She cries out, clinging to my broad shoulders. I take her mouth as I've wanted to do since I landed beside her bed last night. I lay claim to it, consuming her and that sweet taste.

She bites my bottom lip, her nails embedded in my shoulders as she climbs my body. Her legs wrap around my waist, her pussy aligned with my cock.

"Fuck," I growl, her heat searing me even through her skinny jeans. I want them off her. Now. Want nothing between us but the flames scorching everywhere we touch. "Stop me, *mio sole*."

"No."

I yank her shirt off over her head, burying my face between her breasts. They're even more perfect in the light of day, her nipples begging for attention. I'm happy to oblige. I turn my head, dragging one into my mouth.

"Domani!" Her hands land in my hair, pulling. She isn't trying to drag me off, though. Not even close. She wants me right where I am.

I bite and suck, leaving a red mark on her alabaster skin. And then I move to the opposite breast, doing the same. "Stop me," I growl. "If you don't, I won't stop, Finley. I'll take you whether you want me or not."

"Don't stop."

Cristo. My self-control shatters. I fall on her like a ravenous beast.

Her moans fill the little clearing, filtering out into the forest beyond. If anyone is nearby, I'm sure they hear her. I don't give a fuck. This is my property and my woman. If they come near, they'll live just long enough to regret their choice.

"Domani, Domani, please."

"Please, what, *mio sole*? What do you need?"

"More," she whispers through a moan. "I need more."

Who am I to tell her no? She wanted one day to be normal. I can give her more than that. I'll give her utter fucking perfection.

I turn with her in my arms, backing her up against a massive oak a few feet away. Large, flat rocks litter the ground around us, having fallen from the cliff above. I kiss my way down her body, trying to undo her pants at the same time.

Somehow, I manage to strip them and her shoes from her, leaving her in nothing but a tiny pair of panties. They aren't the same ones she wore last night, but they're every bit as innocent. On her, the simple fabric is sexier than lace.

I kneel at her feet, staring up at her in rapt devotion. Yeah, I could spend the rest of my life right here, just like this, and die the happiest motherfucker on the planet at the end of it.

"Domani," she mouths.

I throw her legs over my shoulders, burying my face between her thick thighs.

She cries out, grasping at the tree and my head as if she's afraid I'm going to let her fall. As if she has to worry. She's right where I want her. She isn't going anywhere. I run my nose along the wet spot in her panties, breathing her in. Her heady scent swirls around me, feminine and pure.

I flick my tongue out, dragging it along the seam of her panties. She tastes as good as she smells. Better. I growl, dragging her panties to the side with my tongue as a bolt of lust rips through me. I need her coming on my tongue now. *Cristo.* I can't fucking think until I know what she sounds like when she's falling apart for me.

I spread her legs wide and gorge myself on her. I'm not careful with her. She isn't delicate. I fuck her with my tongue, my hands digging into her thick thighs to hold her still. Her cries of ecstasy fill the clearing, bouncing back from the treetops. Every single one hits me like a shotgun blast, demanding I give her more and more.

I take everything she has, stealing it from her as if it's mine to take. We both know it is, whether she's ready to admit it or not. Her soul, her heart, every inch of her fucking body. They belong to me. I'll leave my marks and my brand all over them. She won't eat or sleep or breathe without thinking about me.

That's her future now. I'm her captor. Her lover. Her world. She doesn't need to see beyond me. I'm all that exists for her.

I thrust my tongue into her tight little fuckhole, using it like a cock to get her off. She rocks against me, riding my face as if she can't help herself. She's a hot little thing, chasing pleasure like it's her job. Right now, it is. It's the only thing she needs to worry about.

I pry her cheeks apart, allowing me to go deeper. I taste her cherry on her, so ripe, so sweet. I want it. It belongs to me.

"Domani. Oh my god."

She's close. I know she is. Her inner muscles flutter around my tongue as she rocks against my face, mindlessly chasing the high.

I grind my nose against her clit, using every part of my face to get her there. I need to see her coming. I need to feel it. Need to revel in it. Fuck. I just need it.

I slip my hand between us, wedging it between her cheeks to play with her perfect little asshole. She shouts when I press against the tight ring of muscle, not trying to breach her entrance but adding one more sensation to the mix.

It's enough.

Her legs clamp around my head, her hands locked in my hair. She soaks my face as she goes off, coming hard. I groan, loving every fucking minute of her surrender. Victory is sweet. It tastes like cherries.

She's still trembling when I drag her down into my arms and rise to my feet. I stalk toward the edge of the spring and wade in. The hot water swirls around my feet and then my legs. I wade deeper, not stopping until it's chest deep.

"Kiss me, *mio sole*," I order, locking her legs around my waist.

She obediently lifts her lips to mine, offering them up eagerly. I devour her, my cock aching where it's wedged between our bodies, trapped against her slick heat. One small shift and the head is right there, nudging against her entrance.

"Stop me," I growl, knowing she won't. Knowing she can't. She's as caught as I am, tangled in a fucking web that might strangle us both. No. It won't. I won't allow that to happen. One way or another, I'm keeping her, and I'm keeping her safe. I'll kill whoever I have to kill, destroy whatever I have to destroy. But this right here—her and I—this isn't some Romeo and Juliet bullshit.

"Domani." She breaks our kiss, lifting her gaze to mine. I can't read her expression. Too much swirls there. But I get lost in her eyes and the hope growing like tiny flames deep within. Every time I look, those flames are brighter, as if her faith has grown stronger the longer she's away from Cillian and that fucking house of horrors.

"Finley," I whisper.

She places her hands on my shoulders, determination flaring in her eyes. Understanding dawns, but it comes a moment too late to stop what she's doing. She slams herself down on me. My hands close around her waist as my cock breaches her little hole and her heat surrounds me. Her hymen tears. We both feel it.

She cries out in pain.

I growl her name in fury and then kiss the sting from her lips. "Foolish little *principessa*."

"I'm sorry," she whimpers. "I w-want to feel it."

"Feel what, *mio sole*?"

"Alive."

I grab her hand, pressing her palm to my heart. "Do you feel this, Finley? So long as it beats, you're alive. You don't have to hurt yourself to feel it. I'll make sure you know every minute that you're still breathing. You'll know joy and laughter and freedom. So long as my heart beats, you'll live."

"I like the way it hurts, Domani."

Cristo. She's going to be the death of me. I know it. It won't take her uncle or Mattia or anyone Rafe Valentino sends after me. Being with this girl will finish me off when nothing else ever could. She's a beautiful, complex puzzle, each piece revealing another startling truth. This one may be the most profound of all. We're not nearly as different as I thought, angel and devil. She craves the dark and all its violent delights, too.

But there's a difference between pleasurable pain sought in carefully defined parameters and that pursued without compunction. If she wants it rough, I'll give her that. But it'll be on my terms, when she's in the right headspace. Not here and now. She needs to learn to appreciate pleasure before she delves into pain. She's had far too much of one and not nearly enough of the other.

"You'll like the pleasure too, *mio sole*," I purr, gathering her long hair up in a loose fist to tip her head back. I drag her bottom lip through my teeth, smiling when she shivers in my arms. "Are you ready to take more?"

"Y-yes."

"Do it. Slow, this time, Finley. Torture me with that sweet cunt before you take me to heaven with it."

"Domani," she moans, her eyes darkening. She does as she's told, though, slowly sliding down on me. She takes me inch by inch, dragging it out until I'm ready to snap. It's exquisite torture, the kind of heaven a man like me won't ever deserve. But I'll fight like hell to keep it anyway.

She moans as she takes me, her head thrown back and her mouth parted in bliss. She's a vision of ecstasy, so goddamn beautiful I can't take my eyes off her. If anyone is out here, I know they can't either. But they can't see anything except her face and the tops of her breasts bobbing out of the water. The rest of her is hidden from view. I feel her, though, every inch of her body gliding against me as she takes me deeper and then deeper still.

By the time her ass comes to rest against my thighs, I'm not sure which of us is closer to breaking. Me? Her? Both of us? The need to move, to fuck and take and consume is overwhelming.

"Please," she sobs, clawing at my shoulders. She draws blood. I fucking love it.

"What do you want, *tesoro*? What do you need?"

"I need you to fuck me."

"No."

She sobs wordlessly, clawing me again. Drawing blood again.

"You know what I want, Finley."

"M-my soul."

"Yes." I smile. "But your secrets will do for now. What were you dreaming about in the car?"

"You."

"Mmm. What was I doing to you? Why were you saying my name?"

"This," she gasps. "You were doing this."

"Talking to you?"

"Fucking me. You were fucking me!" she shouts, lightning crackling in her eyes. "You slipped into my bed, put your hand over my mouth, and took what you wanted. And I loved it!"

There it is. The truth we've both been denying all goddamn day. Part of me wanted to take her...and part of her knows she would have let me. It's twisted and fucked up and wrong on every level there is. But it's what's been festering under the surface since she woke up in my bed.

She isn't afraid of me because her soul recognizes mine. I took her from her uncle because mine recognizes hers. We're two sides of the same coin, and that coin was forged under the cover of night.

I'm the thing monsters fear, hunting men like my father, those who take what they want and leave destruction in their wake. But for her? I'm no better than he is. She's a survivor, refusing to bend to men like her uncle, those who love the pain they cause. But for me? She'd surrender and love every minute of it.

We crave the same twisted thing—the one goddamn thing we shouldn't. Whatever that says about us, it's out in the open now. And there's no taking it back. I'm not sure I would even if I could. I'll bare my soul to this girl, let her see every ugly corner. It won't change a damn thing. When the dust settles, she'll still be mine.

I know because she's here right now, wrapped around my cock and writhing.

She's mine. I know it. She knows it. The fucking universe knows it.

I press my lips to her ear, giving her my truth. "I wouldn't have had to tie you to your bed to keep you there, Finley. When I was taking what I wanted, hell itself wouldn't have dragged you from my arms."

She cries out, her cunt clenching around my cock. I lift her off and then drop her. The water splashes around us. Her moan ripples through the clearing. I do it again and then again.

"Fuck." I drag my lips down her throat. "We may not leave this spring today, *mio sole*. I don't want to leave your body."

"Then don't. Stay inside me until I can't remember what it feels like not to have you in me, Domani. Stay right here forever."

Forever. Now she's speaking my language.

I chase her lips with mine, pulling her into a deep, languid kiss. We fuck the same way, deep, lazily. As if we've got all day. I take my fucking time learning her body, what makes her shake, what makes her beg. She comes for me again and again, moaning, pleading, screaming.

When I know she can't take much more, I give her what she really wants. I clamp my hand down over her mouth and take what I want. I fuck her hard, pounding into her as she claws and fights, pretending like she wants to get away. We both know it's only an act, though. Every time she starts to slip from my arms, she flings herself back into them, as desperate to remain in them as I am to keep her there.

I crane her head back, watching her face as a powerful orgasm rips through her. It knocks her breathless. Her eyes roll back in her head. For a moment, I think she may have passed out, but I hear her muffled screams of ecstasy against my hand and know she's wide awake...living her best fucking life on my cock.

I drag her down onto me, holding her there as the force of her orgasm rips my own from me. My seed shoots down my shaft, spilling into her. I'm not wearing a condom, and I doubt she's on birth control. Our lives are fucked six ways to Sunday. But in this moment, I send up a prayer that it takes root and grows, tying her to me in this way, too.

Chapter Six

Domani

By the time we make it back to the house, Finley is exhausted. I carry her straight to the bedroom, laying her out in the bed. She immediately curls up with my pillow, her eyes fluttering.

"Sleep, *mio sole*. I'll keep watch."

"'Kay," she whispers.

Within minutes, she's out.

I cover her up and stand over her, just watching her sleep. My goddamn heart feels like it's lodged in my throat. Is it possible to fall in love this fast? Once upon a time, I would have said absolutely not. But I've seen love strike like lightning a few too many times to discount it so readily now. There is no rhyme or reason to matters of the heart. Sometimes, you meet your person, and you just know. Other times, love sneaks up on you slowly. Your person is the last one you expected or the one who has been there all along. There is no one way or no right way. There's just love.

I feel it now, rushing through every chamber of my heart. There's so fucking much of it. *Cristo*. It's like an endless wave knocking me down again and again and again. My heart is hers. For as long as it beats, it'll be hers.

I have to find a way to keep it beating.

Fuck, I have to find a way.

I slip out of the room, heading for the office down the hall. I leave the door open as I slip inside, settling behind the desk. It's been a while since I was last here. This place has always felt a little bit like living in exile for me. I don't come unless I have no choice. I'm used to the concrete jungle. It's what I know. It's where I thrive. I've spent my entire life in Chicago, learning every nook and cranny. But today, this place feels a little like paradise, and Chicago feels like the great unknown. It's an odd shift.

I grab my burner from the desk and power it on. Within seconds, dozens of missed calls and texts begin to filter in. I skim the texts, but they're of the same variety I had this morning. Only, Mattia has enlisted help in trying to talk sense into me this time.

Coda: You need to come back, brother. We can handle this as a family.

Diego: JFC, Domani. Are you trying to start a war? Get your ass back here before we have to tell Rafe about this.

Mattia: You're really beginning to piss me off. Answer the fucking phone.

Forty-five minutes ago, Rafe texted.

Rafe: His fucking niece? You're with his fucking niece?? If you haven't called me back with an hour, I'm sending Coda after you.

Cazzo. Coda is my closest friend. He's also the only other hitman on Rafe's payroll. The man knows everything there is to know about the mafia. And he's more dangerous than me by far. But loyalty matters to Coda, and we've been ride or die for years. If Rafe sends him to deal with me, it'll fuck him up in a major way. Rafe knows it, the bastard. And he knows I know it. He's counting on that fact forcing my hand.

I dial his number, cursing him under my breath. Rafe has always been a ruthless, savage motherfucker. He knows exactly where to hit to make it hurt. And he always knows exactly when to strike. It's precisely why we've always gotten along so well. He's a good man...but he can be a downright son of a bitch when he needs to be.

"You kidnapped his fucking niece," he roars as soon as he answers the phone. Rafe doesn't yell often. The fact that he's yelling now means he's more than pissed. "What the fuck were you thinking?"

"I didn't kidnap anyone. She's where she wants to be."

"You strolled out of his goddamn house with a mask over your face and his sleeping niece in your arms," he says. "That's the definition of kidnapping, Brambilla."

"Did you ask him if she was in that house of her own free will?" I ask. "Because I've seen the rope burns on her wrists. And I know how long it's been since she last stepped foot outside. One year, nine months, eighteen days."

"*Cazzo*. You're saying he had her tied up?"

"Not last night," I admit. "But yeah, often enough to leave permanent scars on her wrists."

"*Mafankulo*." If there's one thing Rafe and I have always agreed on, it's that motherfuckers who abuse women don't have a place in this world. They aren't pawns or bartering chips. We're meant to protect and provide, not to terrorize and victimize. Especially not a *principessa*. Irish blood may run in her veins instead of Italian, but she was still born into this life. In his eyes, that makes her princess enough.

"This isn't your fight, Rafe. It's mine. I put the mask on to keep you and the family out of it."

"Yeah, well, you should have checked for cameras in her fucking room," he mutters. "They know exactly who took her. Cillian is demanding a sit-down."

"He had cameras in her room?" I growl, my blood boiling. *Cazzo.* She had no privacy? No escape? Every new thing I learn about Cillian Brennan simply adds one more item to the list of reasons he's going to die by my hand.

"You know that's not our problem," Rafe says quietly. "We stay out of Irish business, and they stay out of ours."

"Yeah, well, you may want to rethink that," I snap, losing my temper with him for the first time in a long time. "The only reason he's in Chicago is because of you. They sent him to take what they haven't been able to get any other way."

"What are you talking about?"

"They wanted a piece of Chicago, and they sent him to pry it from your grasp," I say. "Our plan to have them deal with him? Doesn't fucking matter. According to Finley, his people in Boston know he's skimming off the top and working deals behind their backs. They don't care because he's built a base of power in Chicago. He's become a threat. To you. They're willing to tolerate a lot for that prize."

Rafe mutters a curse.

"So from where I'm sitting, it looks like he has to die either way, Rafe. You can send the family after me for going off-script; that's fine. You do what you have to do. But I'm going to do what I have to do, too."

"What the fuck does that mean?"

"It means I'm going to hunt him down like a fucking dog and end his miserable life. And then I'm going to pick his sons off one by one until the weakest remains. If he agrees to my terms, I'll let him live. If he doesn't, he'll die too. But I'm not giving Finley back to Cillian. Hell will freeze over before I send her back to anyone in that house," I growl, meaning every word. "And if our family gets in my way or tries to stop me, I'll do whatever it takes to protect her."

"You'd choose her over your family? Over your oaths?"

"Yes. And you'd choose Amalia the same way. We both know you would." We both know he did. When it was him, he handed her every shred of evidence she needed to bury him and every single one of us and then sat and waited for the world to burn down around us. The only reason it didn't is because she chose him too.

"*Cristo*, Domani. It didn't have to come to this."

"It did," I say.

"You could have come to me!"

"Had I come to you, would you have helped her? Or would you have sent her back to try to avoid a war?"

He doesn't say anything. He can't.

"My shit can't be your shit when you have the whole goddamn organization to consider, Rafe," I say quietly. "You would have done what you had to do. And I did what I had to do."

"Goddammit, Domani," he growls, his voice rough with emotion I've never heard from him before. This is killing him. I know it is. But I made my choice. It's Finley. And

Rafe has no choice but to make his. I don't fault him for it. I can't. If I were in his shoes, I'd make the same goddamn one. That's the price of being the *capo*. That's what it means to lead.

Uneasy lies the head that wears a crown.

"Don't send Coda," I say. "I don't care who else you send after me, but don't send him."

Rafe sighs...and then disconnects.

I drop my phone on the desk, scrubbing my hands down my face.

That was exactly as hard as I thought it'd be. But I wouldn't do it differently.

My choice was made before I ever carried Finley out of her room. It was her. It'll always be her.

Chapter Seven

Finley

"Wake up, sleepyhead." I smile, running my fingers through Domani's hair. He looks peaceful in his sleep, less like a warrior and more like a slumbering giant. There's a softness to him that's absent when he's awake. I can almost imagine him as a boy. *Almost.* But there's nothing boyish left in this man.

I don't think he meant to fall asleep. He's reclining back on the couch, one foot up on the coffee table with the remote on his chest.

"I'm not sleeping."

"Little liar." My smile grows.

"I'm resting my eyes."

"Well, you've been resting them for a while. And you were snoring."

He cracks one hazel eye open. "I don't snore, *mio sole*," he says, all hot and grumpy. I don't think he's a morning person. Or a waking-up person since it's nearly dusk.

"If you say so, but I'm pretty sure there are bears in the woods planning a protest because you interrupted their hibernation."

I don't sense him moving. I don't see it, either. But the words are barely out of my mouth before his hands are around my waist and he's dragging me down onto his lap.

I struggle in his arms, not trying too hard to get free. He's shirtless, gorgeous, and I'm not crazy. He pins my arms behind my back, subduing me easily.

"Say it now, *piccolina*," he taunts, his cock stiffening against my ass.

"Which part wasn't clear to you, Domani?" I retort, still not afraid of him. Never less afraid of him, actually. I understand him on a fundamental level. I know what makes him tick. I've seen the blackest parts of his soul. And frankly, they captivate me.

"The part where you thought you could be fucking cute and not pay for it by riding my cock right here."

I moan loudly.

He lifts me just high enough to pull his cock from his pants and tug my panties to the side. He didn't bother to dress me before carrying me back to the cabin. He simply wrapped me up in his jacket.

"Keep your hands behind your back."

"I want to touch you."

"I know. You can soon." He runs his thumb up my slit, parting my folds. "*Cristo*. You're wet already."

"Yes, because you're touching me." And because I dreamed of him again. Those dreams pulled me from my sleep, compelling me to his side. I needed him. Needed this. I'm greedy for it, lapping up every touch, every moment, and sensation as if I intend for them to sustain me for a lifetime.

His skillful, wicked fingers dance through my folds, turning me into a pleading, writhing mess. He touches me everywhere except where I need him most.

"Domani, please," I groan. "Please." I can't touch him. He won't let me. And I can't come. He won't let me do that, either. He's tormenting me. Pleasure builds on pleasure, reaching a fever pitch. But there's no relief. There's only the unrelenting agony of anticipation.

"This is the pain you seek in my bed, Finley. This is how we make it hurt," he says. "Understand?"

"Yes!" I sob, willing to agree to anything. Willing to cede anything to him if it means I get to come.

"Good." His cock nudges at my entrance. Before I can take a breath, he's inside me.

I gasp as my body stretches to accommodate him, remembering the heavenly feel of him. He's so fucking big he steals my breath. And I love it.

I love it even more when he immediately starts moving, powering into me with his hands around my arms, locking them in place, and using them to drag me up and down his cock.

I'm not his toy or his plaything. I'm his doll. He uses me how he wants, fucking me like a machine. He's ruthless, merciless. And God, I can't get enough.

"You're such a fucking good girl," he growls, flipping me onto my stomach and yanking my ass into the air. His thumb presses against the tight ring of muscle as he slams back inside me, knocking me breathless. "You fuck like a dream, Finley."

His thumb slips into my ass. My body loses power beneath him, every muscle going lax. He growls, pushing his thumb in and out of me at the same speed he fucks me.

I crumble, scattering to the winds.

"That's it, " he croons. "Come all over me, *mio mostriciattola*." He drives into me again. Again. Again.

I scream, a thousand stars exploding behind my eyelids.

He roars, one hand tangled in my hair, the other gripping my hip. He thrusts deep, so deep I feel the head of his cock against my cervix, and then his seed splashes into me. Hot ropes pulse deep, painting my womb in the evidence of what we are together.

Explosive. Inevitable. *Irrevocable.*

We stay exactly like that for several long moments before he pulls out of me, groaning. A second later, he peels me from the couch, his touch gentle and reverent, as if he didn't just utterly wreck me.

He settles with me in his arms and his lips at my crown. "*Tu mi appartieni, mio sole.*"

"I don't know Italian, Domani."

His lips curve into a smile against my skin. "I know. I said you belong to me."

"I wish that were true," I whisper, meaning it more than I ever thought possible.

He tips my head back, his hazel eyes meeting mine. "Then let's make it true. Marry me."

"What?"

"Marry me, *mio sole*. Now, tonight. Tomorrow. As soon as we can make it happen."

"You want to marry me?" My heart leaps into my throat.

"Your uncle won't be able to touch your money. Neither will I. I'll sign a prenup to ensure it."

My heart falls into my stomach as quickly as it leaped. He doesn't want to marry me. He's just trying to protect me.

"No, thank you."

"You don't want a prenup?"

"I don't want to marry you."

He falls still, his eyes narrowing on me. It might be my imagination, but it looks almost as if pain shoots through his eyes before his expression goes flat. "You don't want to marry me."

It's not really a question, more like a clipped, cranky statement. But I answer anyway. "I'm not tying myself to you just because you think it'll keep my money safe, Domani."

I'm not sure I ever had dreams of getting married. Trapped in my uncle's house, my dreams were far sadder. I dreamed of escape. There were no white knights coming to sweep me away. No fairytale weddings. Even as a kid, I think I knew that wasn't the future waiting for me. Like most women born into this life, I was a tool to be used.

But if I ever did dream of a different life for myself, my future husband didn't tie himself to me out of obligation or a sense of responsibility. He didn't do it because he knew there was a possibility he wouldn't survive the coming days. He did it because he couldn't imagine surviving without me. That's what I want. I won't settle for anything less. With him, I can't. Because I might not have his heart, but I think he has mine.

I don't know anything about love. I don't know what it feels like, what it looks like, or what I'm even supposed to do with it. It's been so long since anyone felt that for me, or I felt that for anyone; it's a foreign emotion, one completely at odds with everything I know. And yet...when I look at Domani? When he touches me? I think it's the thing whispering through me. Those whispers grow louder with every passing moment.

Losing him may kill me. But tying myself to him when he doesn't love me will destroy me in ways far more corrosive. I know pain. I know what it is to lose yourself day by day. I've done it for most of my life. I won't live that way again. I can't.

"Then marry me because I can't fucking live without you," he growls.

My gaze flies to his, shock running through me.

"You heard me, *tesoro*. You think I ask this lightly? I don't." He cups my cheek. "I know what we face. I know what you think. I'm not asking you because I think we're going to die. I'm asking you because I refuse to allow that to happen. You're going to survive this, and so I am. And when it's over, your life will be permanently tied to mine. But in the meantime, your money will be safe. Your uncle will no longer have control over it, and you'll be free."

"Domani," I whisper, hope and fear crashing together like cymbals in my chest. I want to believe him so fucking badly. But do I? Can I? Is there really a future where the two of us walk out of this alive and together?

"*Il mio cuore batte per te.*"

"I still don't know Italian."

"My heart beats for you, Finley." He grabs my hand, laying it flat against his chest. His heart thumps a strong, steady rhythm against my palm, shaking me to my core. "It'll always beat for you. I knew it before I carried you out of your uncle's house last night."

"How?" I whisper. How is he so sure? He's so confident, so unwavering. It's as if he knows beyond a shadow of a doubt that this is what's supposed to happen, as if we're what's meant to be. I want to believe him so damn badly. But I'm terrified to trust the little voice screaming that he's my one. Not because I'm worried that I'll be wrong and he'll lock me away just like my uncle. But because I'm terrified that if I'm right, suddenly, I'll have something to lose. I've never had that before.

"Because you're a piece of me. *Mio cuore. Mio sole. Luce mia.*" His lips brush mine. "*Io e te per sempre.* You and me forever."

I sob, pressing my face to his throat as he cracks my heart wide open and sends my walls crashing to the ground. They fall in a blaze of glory, allowing him to sweep into every space in my heart. I cling to him, tears pouring down my face as years of fear, grief, and rage pour out of me, and the bright sparks of love ignite a wildfire in their place.

"Yes," I manage to whisper through it. "Yes."

Chapter Eight

Domani

F inley and I spend the night at the cabin, making love into the late hours. Eventually, she passes out beside me, too exhausted to hold her eyes open any longer. I let her sleep for a few hours, but I don't. I walk the perimeter of the property, keeping my eyes peeled. Rafe would have had time to get someone to me by now, but if he's sent anyone, they don't show themselves.

I don't count on his mercy. If he can prevent a war and protect the family, he has to do what he has to do. But so do I. And whether he believes it or not, the only way that war doesn't find its way to his doorstep is by killing Cillian. Leaving him alive merely delays the inevitable.

I wake Finley at dawn. We leave the same way we came, with the sun barely cresting the horizon. But I don't head back to Chicago. At least not right away. We head southwest toward St. Louis. I want my ring on her finger before I go back to deal with her uncle.

I take backroads, avoiding the interstate in case Rafe has anyone posted up, looking for us.

Not even halfway there, Finley gets bored of looking at cornfields and cows. There isn't much else in this part of the state. She starts prowling through my shit.

"Jesus, Domani." Her brows climb higher with every weapon she discovers. "How many weapons do you have in this car?"

"Enough," I say grimly.

"How many is enough?"

"As many as it takes to get the job done, *mio sole*."

"How many people have you killed?"

"More than you're prepared to hear."

"Ten? Fifteen?"

"It's more than that, *tesoro*."

"A lot more?"

I nod.

"Five hundred?"

I cut my eyes at her, which makes her laugh. She's fucking with me. That surprises me. "You're not horrified by who I am, are you?"

"No," she whispers, sobering. "I understand you. Maybe better than I'd like to admit. If you're a monster, I'm a monster too. You think I wouldn't do the same thing to people like my uncle if I could get away with it? The people he's hurt don't haunt him. They haunt me. The people you've hurt don't haunt you, but the people they hurt? They haunt you. We're alike, Domani. In every way that matters, we're alike."

"*Cristo*," I mutter. She's so fucking intelligent, it's frightening. Most people aren't emotionally aware. They don't know what they're capable of because they aren't willing to face themselves. She knows because she's not afraid to look deep and examine even the darkest parts of herself. She doesn't run from them. She simply accepts them for what they are.

She knows that dark thoughts and violent delights don't make us monsters because she's faced true monsters. She's lived with evil. She's listened to the screams of its victims and smelled the burning flesh when their pleas fell on deaf, uncaring ears. Darkness balances light. One can't exist without the other. But evil? It's a bottomless pit of hopeless agony and despair. No light will ever burn it out. No good will ever balance it. It exists only to kill and consume. And in the end, to destroy.

We ride in silence for several miles before she grows bored again.

"What are you doing?" I ask, eyeing her warily as she unlatches her seatbelt and climbs to her knees in her seat, a look on her face that I've gotten to know well. She's up to something that's going to get her little ass in trouble.

"Trying something," she says, stretching across the console between us. Her hand lands on my cock.

"Fuck," I groan, slamming my head back against the seat.

"You can stop me if you want. But we both know you don't want." She palms me through my pants, smirking. She's right. I don't want. There's not a chance in hell that I'm telling her no right now.

She unzips my pants, delving her hot little hand inside to drag my cock out. I grit my teeth, trying to keep my eyes on the road instead of on what she's doing. I quickly set cruise control, figuring it's the safest way to keep me from crashing into a fucking tree when she's got her hands on my cock.

"Are you always hard, Domani?"

"When you're nearby? Yeah. Always."

This makes her smile. She wraps her fist around me, gliding it up and down.

"Tighter," I growl.

She squeezes, watching my face to see if she's got it right.

"Yeah, just like that."

She strokes me again. My hands are tight fists on the steering wheel, all of my attention focused on keeping the damn SUV on the road.

"Spit on it, Finley. Get it nice and wet."

"Nah. I think I'll do this instead." She flattens herself across the console, diving for my cock.

"Fuck!" I roar, the SUV swerving sharply as her hot little mouth closes around the head of my cock. I quickly course-correct, swerving back into our lane.

She plunges down, taking me as deep as she can. Choking on me.

I whip the car to the side of the road, slamming on the brakes before I flip it and kill us both. One hand goes to the back of her head, my fingers delving into her hair. I drag her up, forcing her to take a breath.

She fights me like a little hellcat, eager to get back on my cock.

"You want more, *mio sole*?"

"Yes," she hisses.

"Take it."

She does, plunging down on me again and then again. She sucks my fucking soul from my body, humming around me as she sucks and licks and drives me wild. If she's unskilled, so I am. It feels fucking fantastic.

I pump my hips, unable to stay still as she owns me. She likes when I do that. She likes it even more when I hold her still while I do. I fuck her face for a moment, using her to get myself off. She moans around me, trembling.

My balls draw up, my spine tingling.

"I'm going to come, *tesoro*. Do you want it down your pretty throat?"

She bobs her head eagerly.

Fuck, she's perfect.

I groan, pushing and pulling her down on me. My balls give up the fight. I hold her down, growling her name as my seed spills across her tongue and down her throat. She swallows eagerly, drinking every drop I give her.

I watch in rapt fascination, marveling that this beautiful little monster is mine. My heart. My soul. My queen.

I drag her across the console into my arms, taking her lips in a deep kiss. I don't fucking care if she tastes like me. She's mine.

"Mmm," she moans when I let her up for air. "I like this cornfield."

I chuckle, pressing my face to her throat. *Cristo*, she makes me feel alive in a way I never have. "Get your gorgeous ass back in your seat before you see far more of it than you intended, *mio sole*."

She flashes me a grin, scrambling back over the console into her seat. Once she's settled and I've tucked my cock back into my pants, I reach for her hand, lacing our fingers together. She turns a blinding smile on me, her eyes lighter than they've been since she woke in my bed, what seems like a lifetime ago.

I brush a kiss across her knuckles and pull back out onto the road, heading for St. Louis.

I rent a room near the ballpark, paying in cash. Her eyes light up when she throws the curtains open and realizes she can see the Arch from our room.

"I've never been anywhere," she whispers, staring at the Arch with one hand on the glass as if she aches to touch it. "That's what I dreamed about my whole life. Going places. Seeing the world. Just escaping." She turns to look at me. "I've seen more with you in one day than I've seen my whole life, Domani."

I tug her into my arms, brushing my lips across her forehead. When this is over, I'm going to take her everywhere just to see the wonder in her eyes every time she sees some new sight. It's like magic to her. I'll give her the world. Every fucking corner of it.

"Thank you."

I tip her head back, brushing a kiss across her lips. "Don't thank me for taking you from that place, Finley. You didn't belong there."

"I meant, thank you for giving me the last twenty-four hours. It's the first time I've ever felt normal."

"Get used to it, *mio sole*. This is only the beginning."

"I hope so."

"I know so. I won't allow anything to happen to you."

"Then we should probably get moving," she whispers. "The longer he has time to plan, the worse it'll be for everyone."

She's not wrong about that. The longer we give him to make a move, the less time we have to strike first. I intend to be back in Chicago by morning. Which means I need to move fast if I'm getting a ring on her finger today.

"I need to make some calls. Why don't you shower?"

"What kind of calls?"

"We need to get you an ID and a social security card," I murmur. "We'll need them to have a marriage license issued. I know a guy who can make it happen, but I need to track him down."

"Oh. I didn't think about that."

I brush my lips across her forehead. "Go shower, *mio sole*. I'll handle it."

She turns toward the bathroom, but I grab her hand at the last moment, halting her.

"Wait." I pull my phone from my pocket, tuck strands of hair behind her ears, and snap a photo to send to my guy for her ID. "For your ID," I explain when she shoots me a questioning look.

"Oh." She scowls at me. "You could have let me brush my hair, Domani."

"You look beautiful, *tesoro*."

She rolls her eyes but doesn't argue. Instead, she stomps toward the bathroom, muttering under her breath about annoying men. I smile, watching her go. She isn't half as annoyed as she likes to pretend.

Once I hear the shower running, I start making calls.

It doesn't take long to track down my guy.

"You need it this morning?" Aero Doukas complains. "You're asking for a fucking miracle, Brambilla."

"I'm aware. I'm also willing to pay for a miracle. Can you make it happen or not?"

"Depends on whether the police are involved," Aero says. "I can make an ID that'll pass visual inspection to someone untrained, but if a cop gets ahold of it, it's a different story. I need more than a few hours to work that kind of magic."

"The police aren't involved." Cillian can't call them. He can't afford to have them crawling through every inch of his home, not when he's killed God only knows how many people inside. They'd drag him out in cuffs long before they started looking for Finley.

"Fuck. Send me her photo. I'll get what you need," Aero says. "Double the usual."

"When will it be ready?"

"Give me until noon."

"Eleven."

"Noon."

"*Cazzo*," I growl. "Fine."

"Meet at the usual spot?"

"No. The dress shop on Olive Street downtown."

"The dress shop?"

"The bridal shop."

He whistles. "You getting fucking married or something, Brambilla?"

"Something like that."

"Well, goddamn. I'm going to mind my fucking business and not ask any questions before I end up in the middle of some bullshit I don't want to be in the middle of, but congratulations."

A smile touches my lips. Aero is an unusual man, but he's been useful to me over the years. He doesn't work for the mafia. He runs his own thing. We all have our own networks. We never know when we may need them. Sometimes, the best thing we can do for the family is call in outside resources. Sometimes...we need those same resources for ourselves.

No one initiates with plans to betray. Honor matters to every single one of us who swear the oath. It's what keeps us together when everything else is falling the fuck apart around us. But sometimes, circumstances change, and we're forced to change with them. We adapt, or we die.

I'm an adaptive motherfucker.

I'm not a disloyal one, though. Rafe may think I've betrayed my oaths. But I see it differently. I've done everything I could to keep them. I didn't leave to avoid them.

I left to avoid breaking them. And I'm going back for the same reason.

"See you at noon," I tell Aero and then disconnect.

Unlike yesterday, I don't have dozens of missed calls and texts. I have only one from an unknown number.

> Don't go home.

I don't have to ask to know who sent it. I know.

Coda.

Fuck. I guess it's begun, then.

Chapter Nine

Finley

Domani stands beside me in front of the judge, his fingers laced through mine, speaking his vows in that deep rumble I love so much. His voice doesn't waver or shake. He's calm and confident, promising to love, honor, and cherish me for the rest of his days.

When it's my turn to repeat the same words, my voice trembles with emotion. I mean them with every fiber of my being. It's scary how intensely I love this man and how fast it crept over me. But I'm not fighting it anymore, and I'm done questioning it. If he wants my soul, it's his to take. He can have my heart, my body, every inch of me.

He holds my gaze captive as he slips the ring we picked out together on my finger, emotion swirling in his eyes. Tears swim in mine, momentarily blinding me. I don't hear what the judge says after that. All of my attention is on the man in front of me. My husband. My lover. My world.

Somehow, despite the sword dangling over our heads, he made today perfect. I have a dress, flowers, and a beautiful ring. He's in a tux, looking like a freaking model. I never dreamed about a wedding, but this is everything I could have wanted. It's everything.

"By the power vested in me by the State of Missouri, it is my great pleasure to pronounce you man and wife. Mr. Brambilla, you may kiss your beautiful bride."

Domani cups my cheek, stepping toward me. His lips come down on mine. He kisses me with fierce devotion, pouring every part of himself into it as the ladies from the front counter clap politely.

"*Io e te per sempre,*" he whispers against my lips.

"You and me forever," I whisper back in English.

He smiles, pressing his forehead to mine before he wraps me up in his arms. The judge steps forward to congratulate us and then shuffles us off to the side of his desk to sign the license. Within an hour of entering the Marriage License office, we're officially husband and wife. We stop long enough to file the license, and then head out.

As soon as we're outside, he scoops me into his arms, his mouth slanting down on mine again. "You're mine now, *mio sole*," he growls against my lips, his kiss hot and wild, unrestrained. "Mine."

"Then take me to our room and prove it, husband."

"Fuck. Say that again."

"Husband," I whisper.

He practically runs to the SUV with me in his arms. I laugh the whole way, happier than I've ever been.

"Wait," he says thirty minutes later, placing his hand on my arm before I can step onto the elevator. Before I can ask what's wrong, he's sweeping me back up into his arms. "I'm supposed to carry you, *tesoro*."

"That's only over the threshold of our home, Domani."

"No, it's everywhere I say it is."

I smile, touching his cheek. For a man with more blood on his hands than I can comprehend, he's awfully sweet. I love that about him. He is who he is, but his soul is fully intact, untouched by the evil that would have tainted a lesser man than he.

He strides onto the elevator, hitting the button for our floor. Our reflections bounce back from the chrome walls. Him in his tuxedo. Me in my white dress. His olive skin and dark hair like a backdrop for my reds and whites. Somehow, despite our differences, we look as if we fit.

The elevator slides to a stop on our floor. He steps off, moving aside for a middle-aged couple who smile brightly and offer their congratulations.

"We're married," I say as we walk away.

The couple hear me and laugh.

Domani chuckles. "Yeah, we are, *tesoro*."

"I'm a wife."

"Yes. Mine." He dips his head, his lips brushing mine. "And I'm your husband."

"Walk faster," I order him, my core clenching when he says it.

He grins and hurries his pace.

I use the time wisely, nuzzling my face into his throat. Tasting his skin. Dragging my teeth along the tendon of his neck. He growls, his body tense around mine. He's turned on. I feel it pulsing in the air around us like a tangible, living thing.

"You're asking for trouble, *mio sole*."

"No, I'm not asking for anything, Domani." I press my lips against his ear, running my fingers through the hair at the nape of his neck. "I'm *begging* for it."

He growls wordlessly, balancing me between his hard body and the wall beside the door to our room. Within seconds, it's open, and he's storming through. It slams behind us. He pushes me up against it, pinning my hands beside my head.

His teeth sink into the sensitive skin where my neck and my shoulder meet. He wastes no time dragging my dress up my thighs. I'm not a traditional bride, and I didn't pick a traditional dress. The off-the-shoulder number is all lace. The A-Line bottom hits just above the knees, flaring out into a full, fluffy skirt. It's short and daring. I feel like a true princess in it.

I know Domani loves it. He nearly came unglued when I stepped out of the dressing room in it. He's been hard ever since.

"This isn't going to be sweet and gentle," he warns me, dragging the top down to expose my breasts. "I need you too fucking badly."

"Good. Who said I wanted sweet?" I don't. I just want him. There's plenty of time for sweet and gentle later. I know he'll give me that. He'll make me take my time. God knows, he'll take his. Until I'm ready to burst apart at the seams. There is no hurrying Domani. When he decides he wants to make love to me, he sends me to another plane of existence, one singular touch at a time. He did it over and over again last night. The man is a beast in the bedroom, focused solely on me and my pleasure.

But right now, I just want him inside me, claiming me in every way I can be claimed. I want his ring on my finger and his cock inside me. I want his name on my lips and his hands in my hair. I want him. Period.

"Get my cock out," he orders before his teeth close around my nipple. He releases my hands, letting me set to work. I tear through the button on his pants, sending it bouncing across the floor.

Before I have his cock out, he's tearing my panties off...his fingers are inside me. I lose track of what I'm doing. His name falls from my lips in a loud moan.

"Get my cock out, Finley," he demands, delivering a punishing bite to my right nipple. The sting goes straight to my clit. The loud, wet sounds of his fingers moving in and out of me make me wetter, hotter.

I wrap my hand around his shaft, pulling his cock from his pants. It's so beautiful. I don't know if dicks are supposed to be pretty, but his fascinates me. Or maybe that's simply because I know what he can do with it. I know the way it makes me feel. If there's anything in this world better than this man fucking me, I won't survive it.

He lifts me, the head of his cock at my entrance. His eyes meet mine, his expression hot and wild. Full of some emotion I'm not sure I know how to name. Obsession? Possession? Complete capitulation to the bond growing between us? Whatever it is, it's vast and powerful, pulling me under with it.

"*Ti amo, mio sole.*"

I don't know Italian, but I know that one. *I love you.*

He thrusts forward, groaning as he fills me. I don't get a chance to respond. I don't get a chance to process either.

He moves like a storm, fucking me hard and deep. Pounding into me until the door rattles, and I'm screaming his name loud and then louder.

I'm sure half the hotel can hear us. I'm also sure I don't care. Let them.

"*Ti amo*," he growls, his eyes at half-mast as he claims every piece of my soul. "*Ti amo*, Finley."

I splinter apart in his arms, shattering like glass. He falls with me, groaning my name low and deep. I float, caught somewhere between heaven and earth, in that place where forever doesn't seem so impossible after all.

Please, God, don't let it be impossible.

"Did you mean it?" I ask when he pulls me away from the wall, wrapping his arms around me. I hate how small my voice sounds and how vulnerable I feel, but right now, I am small and vulnerable. And I need him to tell me this isn't another dream.

"More than I've ever meant anything. I love you."

"Domani, I..."

He presses his fingers to my lips. "Not yet, *mio sole*."

I lift my gaze to his, not understanding.

"I know how you feel about me, Finley. I feel it when you touch me. But I don't want to hear you say it until you know that we're going to survive this," he murmurs. "That's when it'll be real to you."

"It's real to me now, Domani. *You're* real to me now."

A smile ghosts across his lips. "I know, *tesoro*. But you can't give me all of your heart right now because it isn't whole. Until you know beyond a shadow of a doubt that this isn't the end for you, it won't be whole. When you know that you're truly free and this is just the beginning for you, you tell me how you feel. Until then, I'll wait. However long it takes."

"Domani," I whisper, tears welling in my eyes. What did I ever do to deserve him? How can I ever? He knows me better than I know myself. And he cares for me in a way that no one ever has, even at the expense of himself. I love him with everything I have. And I *hate* that he's right. Part of me can't belong to him right now because that part is still caged up tight, bound in ropes of fear. It never left my uncle's house. Until it does, my uncle still owns it. He still owns part of me.

But I'm so fucking scared that I'm going to lose the man in front of me; I don't know how to let it go. I have something to lose now. Something I need more than I need freedom or life or breath. And that's exactly why my uncle will fight like hell to take it from me.

"I need you to do something for me, *mio sole*," Domani murmurs a while later, running his hands through my hair. "I need you to stay here while I go back."

"No."

"Finley."

"No, Domani." I lift my head, pinning him with a fierce look. "If you go back, I go back."

"Chicago is the last place you need to be right now."

I laugh abruptly. "It's no safer for you. Don't think I don't know what you risked when you took me from my uncle. I was born into this life, too. I know the rules just as well as you do. You betrayed your oath. Your own family will hunt you down and kill you if they find you."

He says nothing, but he doesn't have to say it. I know why he's looking over his shoulder and being so careful. It isn't because he's worried my uncle will find us. It's because he's worried his own people will. He broke the rules when he took me. He interfered in Irish business and left his family open for retaliation. My uncle could start a war over it if he wanted. He likely will.

It's been his plan all along. To find some weakness to exploit. To find some vulnerability to use. He just never anticipated that they'd make the first move by taking me. He won't forgive that slight. Not now, not ever.

"You don't belong in Chicago right now, Finley."

"Well, you can't leave me here. Because if you do, I'll just follow you."

"*Cazzo*," he growls, pinching the bridge of his nose. But he isn't angry. I know he isn't because dark amusement glints in his eyes when he moves his hand. "You would follow me, wouldn't you?"

"Yep."

He shakes his head, sighing. "Fine, *tesoro*. You'll return with me. But you'll do as I say." He hits me with a withering stare. "If you don't and your uncle gets his hands on you, I'll burn Chicago to the fucking ground to get you back, regardless of who gets hurt in the process."

He means it. The truth is right there in his eyes, blazing like unholy fire. This man wouldn't just wage war to keep me. He'd burn the whole world to ash.

Chapter Ten

Domani

"What is this place?" Finley asks, wandering through the safehouse deep in the heart of gang territory. She runs her fingers over the back of the sofa and then trails them along the small bookcase.

"A safehouse," I say, peering through cracks between the boards over the windows at the street below. Cars line the street on both sides, but they're the same ones that were there when we arrived. We weren't followed. "No one knows about it. You'll be safe here."

If there's a safer place in Chicago, I don't know it. I have no ties to this place, no reason to come here. Neither does anyone my family knows about. The apartment belongs to Constantine Attias, an associate of the Arakas family in Silver Spoon Falls. He buried the purchase under a landslide of shell companies to use it the same way I'm using it now, as a place to disappear if the need ever strikes.

When you do what we do, you're always fucking prepared.

By the time anyone untangles the web around this place, we'll be long gone. I'm not making the same mistakes with Finley that Diego did with Amalia, hiding her in an apartment with my name stamped all over it. They can scour every safehouse of mine they can find, but they won't find her. They won't find me either.

We ditched the SUV in St. Louis and rented a Tahoe. I ditched it in a parking garage a few miles from our hotel and bought a nondescript Charger. I barely fit in the motherfucker, but no one knows what we're driving now. It's just another question mark lined up next to a big fucking row of question marks.

I'm not stupid. I've survived this game for a long time. This time, I've got more to lose than ever before. And I don't ever fucking lose. Rafe taught us that.

"Why are the windows boarded up?"

"To keep people out." I shrug. "Fuck if I know. It's not my place."

She stops prowling, turning to me in surprise. "It's not?"

"Nope. It belongs to a friend."

"Oh."

"Come here." I hold my hand out toward her, waiting until she takes it to lead her down the hallway to the bedroom. I turn on lights as we go. The furniture in the place is old and worn, but only a fool fills a place like this with expensive furniture and expects to keep it.

Half of the units in this building are vacant. A third of them are filled with squatters. The only thing keeping them out of this unit is the reinforced steel door and the fact that it's on the sixth floor. If it were easier to get into, all of Constantine's shit would be their shit too. They want somewhere to sleep. This unit is too much of a hassle when there are plenty of others that are far easier to get into.

I pull her into the closet, flipping on the light there.

"What are we... Oh," she whispers when she sees the small door hidden at the back of the closet.

"This is a safe room, *mio sole*." I pull open the panel designed to look like an electric box and punch in the code. The door opens, revealing the real reason I brought her here. The safe room is nearly as large as the bedroom, with its own bathroom and kitchenette. It's also fully stocked and far nicer than the apartment that hides it. "I want you to stay in here."

"Why? I thought you said no one knew about the safe-house."

"They don't, but you'll be far more comfortable in here. And I'll feel a lot better about leaving you here if I know this door is standing closed between you and everyone else in this building. Your uncle and the Valentino family aren't the only dangerous people in this city. They're all around us," I murmur. "And I can't do what I need to do if I'm worried about you."

"I'll stay here," she promises, pushing her way into my arms. "Whatever you need to make sure you come back to me, Domani."

I tip her head up, forcing her to meet my gaze. "I am coming back to you, Finley. All I'm doing tonight is a little information gathering. I won't be gone long."

My promise doesn't soothe the furrow from her brow. It doesn't kill the worry in her eyes, either. That's grown with every mile tonight. I know the only thing that's going to silence it is keeping my promise. She's terrified one or both of us isn't going to make it out of this alive. I'm not going to let that happen, but the only way she's going to believe it is to see it for herself. She's lived with fear for far too long to let go of easily.

I don't blame her for that. How can I? Hope is a fragile thing. People say it doesn't die, but they're wrong. Stifled often enough, it starves. Her uncle has been starving her of hope for years.

No more.

I press my lips to hers, pouring my soul into her for her to keep safe. It belongs to her anyway. It has since the moment I set eyes on her. Perhaps for longer than that. There's a reason I never took anyone to my bed. There's a reason I never imagined a future with anyone until her.

How could I when my soul was forged for her and her alone?

"*Io e te per sempre, tesoro*. I'll be back soon."

"You and me forever, Domani," she whispers back.

I give her the code and wait for her to shut the door between us before I slip out of the apartment.

Coda's sitting on my couch when I slip down the hall, my gun drawn. He doesn't pull his, but I know he hears me. He's got his dark head bent, his hands folded together in his lap.

"I told you not to come back home," he says, not even lifting his head.

"I know. Did Rafe send you, or did you come on your own?"

"Does it matter?"

I slide around the back of the couch so I can see him better, keeping my back to the wall. I know he's the only one here. I checked before I came in through the window. But I'm nothing if not careful. And when your back is up against the wall, you trust no one. Not even your closest, oldest friend.

"It matters," I say quietly.

"He didn't send me," he mutters, lifting his head to pin me with a dark glower. Fury sparks in his green eyes, more emotion than most get from him. Coda can be an ice-cold motherfucker when he needs to be. He doesn't let anyone close. He rarely speaks to anyone. The man is a goddamn wall no one can breach unless he decides to let them. But we've worked side by side for fifteen years. It took him five before he decided he liked me. "He ordered me to sit this one out, but it's fucking you, so I'm here anyway."

"To kill me?"

"Haven't decided yet. I guess that depends on you." He nods at the weapon in my hands. "You going to try to kill me?"

"You know I'm not. We're ride or die, motherfucker."

"Yeah, well, this might be the dying part, motherfuck-er." He blows out a sharp breath. "What the fuck are you thinking, man? This isn't you."

"This is me. You know it is."

Coda knows me better than anyone. He's stitched me up, held my flesh together, and plugged bullet holes with his fingers. He knows the shit I've done and the reasons I do it. He knows exactly who I am and why. He's here now *because* he knows me.

"He kept her locked in that house for damn near two years, listening to every vile thing he ever did. She hasn't known freedom since she was eleven years old. I couldn't leave her there," I tell him. "You wouldn't have left her there either."

"Irish business is Irish business, brother."

"*No, fanculo quello*," I growl. "This city belongs to Rafe. It belongs to the Italians. What happens in it is our business. It's always been our business. The only reason he's here now is because he's trying to take what doesn't belong to him. And the only reason Rafe is letting him is because he doesn't want to face another war. But wake the fuck up, Coda. Cillian's been preparing for war since he set foot in this city. That's the only reason he's here."

"They don't have the numbers to survive a war."

"Are you so sure about that?" I ask. "Because I'm not. Finley isn't. She's lived in that house, listening to him spew his bullshit day in and day out for nearly two years now. He's been growing his ranks and prepping for war since he arrived in Chicago. And we let it happen right under our goddamn noses because we're too busy with our own bullshit to pay attention."

Coda eyes me, uncertain for the first time since I stepped through the door. He isn't stupid or slow. He knows everything there is to know about the *La Cosa Nostra*. And I'm guessing he's picked up more than his fair share of knowledge about the Irish mob too. He knows if I'm telling him that war is coming, I'm not just making it up to save my own ass. He knows far too much to believe something that fucking ridiculous.

"Did Rafe have the sit-down Cillian wanted?"

"He agreed to it. Cillian didn't show."

"Why the fuck wouldn't he show?" I ask, my brows furrowing. "He demanded it."

"Don't know. Every conversation he's had, he's had outside. We haven't heard a word that he hasn't wanted us to hear. Mattia figures he suspects you planted devices somewhere in the house."

"*Cazzo.*"

"Our best guess is that he didn't show today because he's already made up his mind on how he's going to proceed." Coda eyes me levelly. "We're preparing for war and hoping we're wrong, brother."

"Why are you here, Coda?"

"You know why."

I close my eyes, muttering a curse. "No."

"It's not your choice to make, brother. It's mine."

"Yeah, well, you're making a shit choice if you're here right now instead of there." My eyes flash open. I pin him with a withering glare. "Because they need you. I don't. The only thing you're liable to do here is paint a fucking target on your back too."

"We ride together, we die together." He grins, a cold-blooded, merciless grin. "But I'd like to see that son of a bitch howling for mercy before we die, wouldn't you?"

"It's the number one item on my to-do list." I pause. "But I'm not just taking him out. I'm taking out his sons, too. The only one I'm leaving alive is the one who begs the loudest."

"Sounds like a good time to me."

I sigh, shaking my head. I don't want him to do this. If he does, there's no guarantee he'll be welcomed back. Like me, he'll be defying a direct order and betraying his oath. There's no room in the mafia for men who can't fucking take orders. There's no room for men who can't keep their word. Failing to punish one leaves the door open for others to do the same.

But this is Coda. The most dangerous motherfucker in the mafia. And the one person I'd trust to watch my back against any comer, any time, any place, any day. If anyone can help me kill that son of a bitch and stop him from starting a war, Coda can. I need him on this, even if it costs him everything, too.

"Fine. Let's go kill my wife's uncle," I mutter.

Coda's brows shoot toward his hairline. "Hold on. You got married?"

"Today."

"*Cristo.* Rafe is going to shit a brick."

"No," I say quietly. "That's the one part of this Rafe would understand. Let's get the fuck out of here before Diego gets bored of sitting in his car and decides to come in to poke around."

"You saw him out there?"

"He wasn't exactly trying to hide."

Coda lifts his chin in acknowledgment. "No one wants to be doing this shit, Domani. You're family. It's a shitshow all the way around."

"Yeah, well, I made my bed."

"Was it worth it?"

"No question, brother. No question."

Chapter Eleven

Domani

Cillian's compound isn't dark and silent this time. Every fucking light is on, almost as if they're afraid of the bogeyman. He even has guards posted at the front door. I'm guessing he has another at the back.

"Killing him somewhere else would be easier," Coda mutters from beside me. "Who knows how many people he's got inside the house?"

"True, but he didn't let her leave here. Why should he get the opportunity? Besides, he has an incinerator in the basement."

"Jesus fucking Christ." A look of disgust crosses Coda's face. "He burned bodies with her in the house?"

"He did worse than that."

Coda grunts, his contempt obvious. We watch the house for a good hour, not speaking. The guards don't leave the front porch. They aren't particularly observant, either. They don't check the perimeter. They just fucking sit around, talking.

"If the guard around back is anything like these two, getting in won't be a problem," I mutter.

"Nope," Coda agrees. "When are we going in?"

I consider telling him right now. I want this shit over and done with. But everyone in the house is still up from the looks of it. And I want this to be as easy as possible. I don't want to fight my way through Cillian, his four sons, and whoever the fuck else is inside. I want to catch them while they're sleeping. Sooner or later, the motherfuckers have to sleep.

"As soon as we're sure Cillian and his sons are the only ones inside," I say.

"That won't be tonight. It'll be dawn soon."

"I know. *Merda.*" I scrub a hand down my face, fucking exhausted.

"Have you slept?"

"Not much. Not enough," I admit.

"Go. I'll keep an eye on the house and trail him if he leaves. You get a few hours with your wife and meet me back here at sundown. If we're lucky, he'll be dead tonight."

"You know Rafe and Mattia will be looking for you today."

"Yep."

"What are you going to tell them?"

"The truth. You aren't my enemy, and we want the same fucking thing. If Rafe and Mattia need to handle me when the dust settles, so be it."

"So be it," I sigh.

"You're back!" Finley cries, flinging herself at my chest as soon as I step through the door into the safe room. I don't think she's sat down once. The bed is still perfectly made. The chairs are still pushed up to the table. She's probably been pacing since I left.

I drag her into my arms, slanting my mouth down over hers. I kiss her until neither of us can breathe, not sure if I'm trying to soothe her mind or my own.

"I told you I was coming back, *mio sole*."

"I worried anyway."

"I know." I run the back of my hand down her cheek, smiling gently. "But I have news."

"He's dead, and we get to live happily ever after?"

"Not yet."

Her nose scrunches.

"I won't be going into his place alone. I'll have a friend watching my back."

"A friend? From the mafia?"

"Yes."

"I'm not sure if that's good news or bad news, Domani."

I'm not sure, either. I trust Coda implicitly. He wouldn't betray me. But the fact that he's risking everything to do this with me worries the fuck out of me. Either things are far worse on the home front than I suspected, and Rafe still thinks he can stop this war despite all the evidence saying he can't, or Coda has reason to believe we won't survive a war. It's a grim fucking prospect either way.

But Coda didn't betray his oath just because we're ride or die. He did it to protect the Valentino family, the same way he's always protected them. He has his debts to pay to Rafe, too.

Regardless of his reasons, I need him in my corner. And regardless of what Rafe thinks, killing Cillian is the right choice. His buddies in Boston might be pissed about it. His flunkies here might be pissed too. But by the time they can rally to install a new leader, we'll already have his son installed. And he'll play by whatever rules Rafe wants to set, or Rafe can snatch every corner of Chicago out of his grasp. His choice. I don't really give a fuck what Rafe decides. So long as Finley is safe, the rest is just noise.

I just need to survive long enough to see the shit through.

"It's good news, *tesoro*."

"Okay. If you say so." She lays her head against my chest, sighing.

"Are you hungry?"

"Not really."

"Come shower with me then."

"Uh, I've been in that bathroom, Domani. There's no way we're both fitting in that shower. It's tiny."

"We'll fit." I tug her hand to get her moving, propelling her through the small space. Once we're in the bathroom, I start the water and quickly strip her. Within seconds, steam swirls around us, fogging up the mirror. I run my lips across her shoulder before stripping my own clothes off.

She squeals when I boost her into my arms, carrying her into the shower.

"Told you that we'd fit, Finley." I press her back against the wall. There's no way I can fuck her in here, but that's not why I wanted her in here in the first place. I just wanted her naked, soapy, and in my arms. Any opportunity I have to get her naked, I'm taking.

"Barely."

I run my lips across her cheeks, her eyelids, her lips, raining kisses across her gorgeous face. I touch her everywhere I can reach, long strokes of my fingers down her arms and sides, and then up her legs. She melts beneath me, purring like a happy little kitten as her worry fades, relaxation setting in.

"What are you doing to me, Domani?"

"Making you forget everything but me," I murmur, tipping her head back to wash her hair. She purrs louder, reveling in every touch. It kills me in a way that she's never had that before now. I think I'd kill anyone who put their fucking hands on her before me. But I hate that she's been starved for affection as much as she has been starved for hope. She deserved both. "Would you like to know a secret, *mio sole*?"

"What?"

"There was never anyone before you."

Her eyes flutter open, a womanly smile curving her lips. "I know, Domani."

"You know?"

"I know you've never been with a woman because you would never give your body to someone when your soul belonged to another. And that's always been mine. You knew it even before you found me."

Cristo. She knows me so well it should terrify me. But it doesn't. The way this beautiful little monster makes me feel is nothing short of utter perfection. I don't deserve it. God knows I've destroyed lives and broken homes and ruined men all over this city. But if there's salvation for me, it's right here in her arms. It's in her eyes. It's in the way she smiles at me as if she sees every piece of me and finds every piece worthy.

I dip my head, taking her mouth in a reverent, worshipful kiss. Even though it wasn't my intention, we end up fucking against the wall of the shower.

I sleep for four hours before my eyes spring open. Finley's still sleeping peacefully at my side, but I'm wide awake. I crawl from the bed and power on my burner phone to check in with Coda.

As soon as it's up, notifications start rolling in.

The same unknown number Coda contacted me on previously pops up.

> He's up to something. There's a lot of movement in the house and on the street out front.

Half an hour later, he sent another text.

> He's on the move. I'm going to follow him.

Fifteen minutes later, he tried to call me.

That was two hours ago. He hasn't been in contact since.

> **Me: You good?**

He doesn't respond.

I dial the number he called me from, but it goes straight to voicemail.

Fuck. Something is wrong. Coda would have sent a message to let me know all was well. We've done this far too long to leave that question up in the air. When someone doesn't check in, it's never good news.

My suspicions are confirmed two minutes later when I receive a text.

> His life for my niece. Bring her to me, or I kill him.

I don't even hesitate before dialing Rafe's number.

"Have you heard from Coda?" I ask as soon as he answers.

"No, but I'm guessing you have if you're calling me."

"*Cazzo*! That motherfucker has him."

"Who?"

"Cillian."

"How do you know this?"

"He was tailing Cillian this morning, Rafe. He hasn't checked in since, and I just got a text saying his life for Finley."

Dead silence echoes down the line before Rafe curses softly. "I'd hoped he'd make a different choice."

"He made the choice he did to protect the family, fully aware that you might kill him for making it. He knows war is coming, Rafe. He was trying like hell to help me stop it."

"It wouldn't be coming if you hadn't started it."

"That's not true, and you know it. Do you really think Coda would have sided with me if I was the one who put the family in danger?" I ask. "This thing with Cillian was going to end up here one way or another. I'm just the excuse he's using. Coda sees it. I see it. Why can't you?"

He doesn't say anything.

"It's not your fault, Rafe," I press on, knowing damn well that I might just push too far. But if I don't say it, no one else will either. I know why he's so fucking reluctant to see what's right in front of his face. Because if he does, he has to face the fact that he fucked up. And after everything else we've been through, the last thing he wants to admit is that this happened because he wasn't paying close enough attention. The last thing he wants to face is the possibility that everything he's done over the last few years to stave off war means absolutely nothing because he missed the one brewing right under his nose.

"You weren't the only one responsible for paying atten-tion," I say. "We all were. We all should have seen what was happening, but we were all fucking busy dealing with all the other bullshit coming our way. That doesn't make you weak. It doesn't make you a shit leader. It makes you fucking human. But what you do now? That defines who you are. You can either wait until it you have no choice, or you can show him who the fuck he's dealing with."

"*Cristo*, Domani," Rafe growls. "When the fuck did you start talking so goddamn much?"

"When you decided to put me in charge of some of this bullshit. You asked me to step up and lead. I stepped up."

"If we're doing this, we aren't doing it divided. You bring the girl here, Domani. We decide as a family how we're going to handle this shit."

"I won't give her back, Rafe. She's my wife."

"*Cristo*. Of course you married her."

"I did. If that changes things, so be it."

"It changes nothing, Brambilla," he says, wry amusement in his voice. "Bring her here. We'll figure it out together."

"I want your guarantee that she'll be protected."

"You know she will."

"That's not good enough, Rafe. I know I betrayed my oath and defied direct orders. I know you have to do what you have to do about that. If you kill me for it, so be it. But regardless of the outcome, I want to know that she'll be protected."

"I vow to you that she'll be protected no matter what, Domani," he says, his voice somber.

I exhale a breath.

"Now, fucking come home so we can go get Coda. And then I can kill you both for pissing me off."

"Yeah. We'll be there," I promise, disconnecting.

I drop the phone and turn around.

Finley's standing beside the bed, her wide eyes and stricken expression telling me louder than any words that she heard far more of that conversation than I ever intended for her to hear.

Fuck.

Chapter Twelve

Finley

"**F**inley, *mio sole*." Domani takes a step toward me, his hand outstretched as if he's asking me to take it. For the first time since I met him, I refuse. I heard most of his conversation. I should have told him I was awake, but I didn't.

All this time, he's been telling me that we're going to make it out of this alive. He's said it over and over again, as if he has no doubts. And now, he's just going to turn himself in to Rafe Valentino and let the chips fall where they will.

I know he's doing it to ensure I survive. But I don't want to survive this if he doesn't. He's my safety. He's my peace. Without him, it means nothing. I thought I'd rather die free than live imprisoned in hell. But if the choice is between letting him die or chaining myself in hell to keep him breathing, I'll lock the chains around my throat myself.

He doesn't get to make that choice for me. My whole life, my choice has been taken from me, stripped by a man who was supposed to protect me. I won't allow this one to do the same thing and call it love.

"Don't touch me, Domani," I growl, my voice shaking.

"Finley."

"You don't get to decide for me what I'm willing to risk. You don't get to decide what I'm willing to accept. You don't get to strip my choice away and say it's for my own good. If that's what you call loving me, you can take it straight to hell, Domani," I cry. "I get to decide for me. *Me.* And I didn't choose to risk your life to save my own."

He stands quietly, listening. "You're right, *tesoro.* That isn't my choice to make."

"Then stop trying to take it from me. If there's even a slight chance that Rafe Valentino is going to kill you, we aren't going there."

"We have to go, Finley," he says quietly. "If we had another choice, I wouldn't even consider it. You know I wouldn't. But your uncle has Coda. He's going to kill him if I don't turn you over. Rafe is the only one who can help ensure that I get Coda out of there alive and keep you safe, too."

My heart stalls in my chest, puttering out. "He has your friend?"

"Yeah, *mio sole*. He has him."

Then he's right. This isn't about me or my choices anymore. This is about a man's life. I can't let his friend die to keep myself out of my uncle's hands. I can't live with that on my conscience. And I can't ask Domani to live with it on his either. We have to go see Rafe, even if it means I might lose him.

No. I won't lose him. I refuse to accept that outcome. I don't know if we get to manifest our own destiny, master our own fate, or tell God what we want for our lives. But I've spent ten years under my uncle's thumb, slowly losing myself, slowly fading away. I've been to every level of hell there is and live with those sounds and smells and memories plaguing my mind. I'm owed one answered prayer. I'm not greedy. I'm not asking for anything more than that. Just one is all I want. And it's this: for the two of us to survive and thrive and find our happily-ever-after together.

If God can't give me that, then I'll take it for myself. Because I'm not just letting life happen to me anymore. I'm not locked in that house. I'm not a victim. I'm not helpless. And I'll fight whoever I have to fight to keep this man breathing.

We're going to survive. I won't accept anything less.

"Domani?"

"Yeah, *tesoro*?"

"I love you."

He stares at me, not moving, not blinking. Not even moving. For a long, silent moment, he just stares. And then he's charging toward me like a wild beast. He plows into me, knocking me backward onto the bed, his hand behind my head to keep it from bouncing.

"You mean it," he says, coming down on top of me, pinning me beneath him. "You believe we're going to survive."

"No. I know we are."

The sheer joy in his kiss is infectious. This man. God, this beautiful, beautiful man.

"I'm sorry I yelled at you," I whisper as he pulls into the driveway of the Valentino mansion.

"Don't be sorry, *mio sole*." He lifts my fingers to his lips. "Never stop defending yourself and what you deserve that fiercely. If I'm doing something that hurts you, you tell me just like that. You never stop telling me like that. You've been silenced too long. Never hold any part of yourself back to spare me. Understand?"

"Yes."

He parks in front of the mansion. I peer up at it, my stomach churning. It's drastically different from Cillian's rundown mansion. The grounds are immaculate. The house is overwhelmingly large and ostentatious. Ivy clings to the white walls, making it seem more like a castle than a home. But I don't think it was built in love.

"I don't like this place, Domani."

"Me either," he mutters. "No one does. Rafe's father wanted the biggest house in Chicago. He succeeded, but it feels like a mausoleum. Not even Rafe likes this house."

"Why does he stay?"

"Because it's the only place that still holds memories of his mother."

"Oh," I whisper, my heart panging in empathy for the man I've heard so much about but have never seen. I know what it is to lose a parent. My mom died giving birth to me. And then my dad was murdered. I didn't get to cling to our house. Instead, I clung to my uncle. By the time I realized I was clutching a monster, it was too late to save me.

"I want you to stay close, Finley. But if things go bad, run to Amalia. She'll make sure you're safe."

"Domani."

"Promise me, *mio sole*."

"Fine. I promise," I snap, angry all over again that he's risking his life for mine. I know we're going to survive because I won't accept anything less. But that doesn't make the situation suck any less.

He runs his fingertips down my cheek. "I know how much I'm asking of you by asking you to walk in there with me, *tesoro*. I don't ask it lightly."

"Can we please just get on with it before you make me cry?" I ask, my chin quivering. I need to walk in there as a *banphrionsa*, with my head held high...someone they can see as Domani's equal. If I walk in as a sobbing wreck, they'll never see me that way. To them, I'll always be the poor little Irish girl he rescued. He needs a queen, not someone they pity.

"In a minute, *bellissimo mostriciattola*." He pops open the glove compartment, fishing out the small knife he hid there when we changed cars in St. Louis. "I want you to put this in your pocket."

"What? Why?"

"Because it won't take long before your uncle knows we're here. I'm sure he has people watching. If he shows up or anything goes wrong, I want you to be able to protect yourself."

My hand closes around the knife. It's a foreign weight in my hand, one completely unfamiliar to me. Cillian always kept his weapons where I couldn't get to them. I think he worried I might use them on him. Domani shows me where the release is on the knife and makes sure I know how to open and close it before I slip it into my pocket.

"Now, we can go," he says, killing the engine. He brush-es his lips across mine before climbing from the car and circling around. I watch the house, but no one comes out to meet him. It's as if they're waiting for him to come to them. Because it's a trap? I hope not.

He helps me out and then guides me up the steps, his hand on the small of my back. I don't try to lace my fingers through his, not wanting to slow him down if he needs to reach for a weapon. I pray it doesn't come to that. But everything I know about Rafe and his family, I learned from my uncle. He wasn't exactly a reliable narrator.

Domani raps on the door.

My heart lodges in my throat. I think it may stay there until we leave this place.

"*Io e te per sempre,*" he murmurs.

"You and me forever," I whisper back.

The door opens. The man behind it doesn't even look at me; his cold gray eyes settle on Domani. He's a few years older than the man beside me and infinitely harder. If Domani is steel, this man is chromium, the hardest metal on earth. He's also furious with my husband.

"Domani," he says, his voice the dangerous rumble of a waking giant.

"Mattia." Domani doesn't bow to him. He meets him as an equal, uncowed and unafraid. I don't think anything or anyone scares my husband.

"Hello," I say politely, inserting myself into their stare-down. "It's nice to meet you, Mattia. I'm Finley."

Mattia's eyes fall to me and the hand I've extended toward him. His expression softens incrementally, and I know he's seen the rope burns on my wrist. That wasn't my intention, but there's no hiding them now. They're a permanent part of me, my wrist rubbed raw too many times for the skin ever to be the same again.

"Hello, *piccola*," he says, his tone softer too. But he doesn't take my hand. I think maybe that's out of respect for Domani? I'm not sure. "It's nice to meet you." He holds the door open for us to enter. "Rafe and Luca are in his office."

"Where are Gabriel and Diego?" Domani asks as we step inside.

"Retracing the trail they got from the tracker in Coda's car." Mattia leads us through the house. There are men scattered around everywhere, all pretending not to be paying any attention to us. They're well-trained, but it's obvious they're listening.

There are warm touches throughout the house. Photographs on the mantel and the walls. Bright pops of color scattered here and there. It's stunning; there's no denying that. But Domani is right. Not even the warm, homey touches hide the fact that this place feels like it has no soul.

There's happiness here. I feel it around us. Even with the tension in the air, the softer emotion still lingers, as if someone just laughed in the room before we walked in. But underneath that, it's...dead. If Rafe's father poured any love into building this place, it died a long time ago.

Mattia raps on a door midway down the hall and then steps aside for us to enter. Domani goes first as if to ensure it's safe for me. He steps inside and looks around before holding his hand out to pull me over the threshold.

I'm too busy looking at all the books scattered on shelves around the room to notice the two men standing beside the massive desk at first. But as soon as my gaze lands on them, wonder turns to worry. They're both grim-faced and silent. They're definitely brothers. They share the same dark features.

But I was wrong earlier. Mattia isn't the hardest man I've ever met. The brother on the right is. He was forged from titanium. He's beautiful. And dark. And I think he may be the most dangerous man I've ever met. He must be Rafe. Which means the other brother—the one who still knows gentleness—is Luca.

"Domani," Luca says.

"Luca."

"Domani," Rafe growls.

"Capo." Domani dips his head, showing respect he hasn't given to anyone else. He's met them as equals. But this man, he meets with a show of deference.

Rafe turns his dark eyes on me. I press closer to Domani as he scours my expression, reading everything that shows on my face. I try to hide it, but he sees right through me. I think he may see clear to my soul. This man is not one to be trifled with.

But I'm not afraid of him. I let him see that, offering it up willingly. He may be the king of kings here, but I no longer bow to anyone. Not now. Not ever again. Not even to this man.

A tiny smile curves his lips up at the corners. Amusement glints deep in his dark eyes. "Hello, *principessa*. It's nice to finally meet you."

I consider lying to him to be polite, but I think he'd rather choke on the truth than dance with a lie. "Hello, Rafe. I wish I could say the same for you, but this is the last place I want to be right now."

His smile grows. "Honesty. I appreciate that."

"I figured you would."

"Why don't you want to be here, *principessa*?"

"Finley," Domani murmurs, cautioning me to tread carefully.

"I know a thing or two about leaders, Rafe. My father was one. He knew when to be the hammer and when to be the nail, when to listen and when to speak. Leaders know when to lead...and when to follow. They're capable of both because they're secure in their place. They don't have anything to prove to anyone, and they don't cling to power because they don't need it," I say, holding his gaze.

"But I also know a thing or two about weak men who play at being leaders. I know they're willing to do whatever it takes to ensure no one questions their authority. I know how far they'll go to make themselves look powerful and how much destruction they're willing to leave in their wake. I know this because my uncle is one of those men." I pause. "I'm just not sure which you are."

The amusement fades from Rafe's eyes, but he doesn't say anything. No one else speaks either.

"My husband defied your orders," I murmur into the silence. "He carried me out of my prison and ensured my captor couldn't get his hands on me again, even after you demanded he return. Your rules say you have to punish him for that. But if you're a leader, you make your own rules. So make your own rules, Rafe. Because I'll chain myself in hell before I allow you to kill him. He doesn't die just so I can live. I refuse to accept that."

"That's enough, *mio sole*," Domani says, placing his hand on my arm. He tugs me backward. "You've said enough. Don't castigate him for doing what he must to protect this family. We've been through battles you don't understand. He makes the choices he does because he has no choice. To do anything else puts everyone at risk."

"And you made the choice you made because you had no choice," I argue, frustrated. "It's always kill or be killed with you guys. There is no compromise, no finding a better way. You cling to old laws and old ways out of tradition even when those old ways no longer serve you. The mafia doesn't change. Irish, Italian, Russian, it doesn't matter. You're all the same, so steeped in tradition you're choking on it. And it'll kill all of you before you even wake up and realize that it's happening."

I had no say in my imprisonment. But they put the chains on themselves. And even now, they refuse to stop pulling them tighter.

Chapter Thirteen

Domani

F inley retreats to the far side of the office, staring out at the backyard. I don't know what she's thinking, but I know she's angry. At me. At Rafe. Perhaps even at life.

I don't know what Rafe thinks about what she had to say, either. He doesn't address it. He simply circles around his desk and sits, getting down to business.

"This is the path Coda took today," he says, turning his laptop around to show me the screen. Coda started at Cillian's and drove several miles before stopping. He then retraced his path two miles before stopping again.

"He called me from there. The timestamp matches."

Rafe zooms in on the area, but it's nothing but an abandoned warehouse.

"Whatever happened either happened inside or on the road outside," Mattia says.

"An ambush?"

"Most likely. Coda wouldn't have followed them into a warehouse."

"Agreed," Rafe says. "Someone let Gabe and Diego know this is the spot where it happened."

"Already on it," Luca says, already typing out a text.

"Where does the tracker go from there?"

"Back to the house."

"They're holding him there?"

"Looks like it."

"*Fottuti idioti*," Luca mutters, tossing his phone on the desk.

"Have you picked up anything on the devices yet?"

"Nothing."

"*Cazzo*. He must have swept the house for them."

"Either that, or they just aren't fucking talking anywhere near where you planted them."

"I put them in every common room in the house, including the office and the damn downstairs bathroom."

"That explains the unholy noises I heard last night," Mattia mutters.

"So we're hitting the house?" Luca asks.

"No."

Everyone looks to Rafe.

"We have no idea how many men he has inside. We need to draw as many of them out as we can. We're splitting into two teams. One will meet Cillian for a fake hostage exchange. The other will advance on the house to clean it out." He meets our gazes, his level. "No one walks out alive from either the house or the hostage exchange. No one."

Fake hostage exchange. Cristo. I knew it was coming. I knew since the minute I got that fucking text. But I'd hoped like hell that there was a different way, some way that didn't require us to dangle Finley in front of that motherfucker like bait. I don't want her anywhere near him, let alone breathing the same air in the same room while bullets fly.

It's dangerous. Everything in me screams to protect her. But this time...I fucking can't. Because the best way to ensure she's never in danger again is to put her in danger now. It's a hell of a problem.

But we have no choice. To set her free, we have to risk it.

"You sure about that?" Mattia asks. "They'll only send someone else to take his place if you don't decide for them who it's going to be."

"Let them," he growls. "They won't get a fucking inch of this city. It belongs to us, and we're not sharing it. Not after this bullshit. If they line them up, we'll keep knocking them down for however long it takes for them to get the fucking point." His gaze briefly bounces to mine as if in silent acknowledgment of the conversation we had earlier. "This city belongs to us. We're not sharing it."

I nod. There can be only one king in Chicago. We've already crowned ours. If the Irish mob wants a new territory to play in, this one isn't it. We have far too many problems already. Between the gangs, the families, the feds, and the fuckery constantly hitting us from every side, we don't need the Irish or the Russians or anyone else trying to add more fuel to the fire.

Somewhere on the horizon is peace. That's what we're trying to build here. That's what Rafe wants for everyone so desperately. Peace. A chance to fucking breathe. But we'll never get it if we're constantly fending off every other fucking mob who thinks they can take what belongs to us.

We've already taught our people the painful lessons they had to learn to get the fuck in line. I guess it's time to teach everyone else. They can't have Chicago. They can't have Finley. And if I have to leave a goddamn pile of bodies for them to learn the lesson? Well, I've always been good at murder and getting away with it.

"I like her for you," Rafe says an hour later, eyeing me across his desk.

He kicked everyone else out. Finley didn't want to leave. I had to promise her that I'd be okay. She glowered at Rafe on the way out, as if silently daring him to try something.

My wife is fierce when she's feeling protective. I never thought I'd live to see the day a tiny Irish princess decided I needed her protection, but here we are. I fucking love her for it.

"I like her for me too."

"Amalia and Callandria will love her. Genesis, too, for that matter. She's a fucking warrior just like they are."

"Around here, that's what it takes."

"Yeah." He sighs. "You know she has to go with us when we meet her uncle. He won't show if she isn't there, and our plan will fall apart."

"Fuck." I scrub my hands down my face. "I know."

"You know I'll do everything I can to ensure he doesn't get his hands on her."

"I know," I growl.

"But if we don't make it out..."

"I know," I snap, glaring at him. "You think I don't? I haven't thought of anything else since you made the plan, Rafe. It's driving me fucking crazy. But I'll follow through because there is no other choice. We can't leave him alive, and this is the best shot we have of taking him out without getting everyone killed. Doesn't mean I fucking like it."

He nods, understanding better than anyone how this shit feels. He's been here. Tommaso Genovese kidnapped his wife. We decimated his ranks to get her back, and then Rafe put a bullet in his head. The fact that he had her ate him alive. If anyone knows what hellfire burns me right now, he does.

"She wasn't wrong."

I meet his gaze.

"What she said earlier," he clarifies. "She wasn't wrong."

"I know. She rarely is." We do cling to tradition even when it threatens to destroy us. It's the thing I hate the most about this fucking life. In a lot of ways, it never changes. It's the same shit, different day. But she was wrong, too.

Rafe isn't old school mafia, immutable and unchanging. He and his twin, Nico, watched their mother die on a sidewalk when they were kids. It changed him. He's turned tradition on its head a thousand times over since he took charge, enforcing new ways and new rules, even when he's had to drag the families along kicking and screaming. He's molded us into one singular organization, into one family. If anyone can keep the ship from going down in a world where men like us and ships like ours sink every day, it's him. That's why he has my respect and my loyalty. That's why I follow him.

"Tell her I don't have any plans to kill you, Domani," he says. "I never did. I'm not a complete fucking idiot. I need you alive far more than I need more power." He shoots me a withering glare. "But don't for a single fucking minute think that you're off the hook because you aren't. As soon as this shit is over, you and Coda are going to wish you were dead. Every fucking miserable job that needs doing, you two will do. Every errand, every body that needs to be buried, every skeleton that needs to be dug up, and every drop of blood that needs to be cleaned up, I'm calling you. And you'll answer. If you don't, I'll hunt you down myself."

"Fair enough," I agree, willing to give him that.

"One more thing," he says when I push myself to my feet. "When you kill her uncle, you make damn sure it hurts like hell."

"Already planned on it."

"Good."

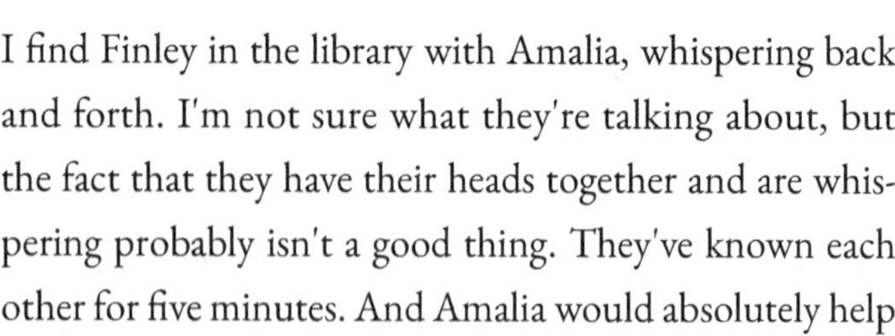

I find Finley in the library with Amalia, whispering back and forth. I'm not sure what they're talking about, but the fact that they have their heads together and are whispering probably isn't a good thing. They've known each other for five minutes. And Amalia would absolutely help

Finley destroy the world. Queen or no queen, she's a little monster herself.

As soon as they see me coming, they sit up straight.

"*Reginetta*," I murmur, dipping my head to Amalia. "*Mio sole*. What are you two doing?"

"Nothing," Amalia lies.

"None of your business," Finley says.

I smile, shaking my head. Yes, these two together are definitely going to be a problem. But it's good to see Finley at ease in this house. It's the first time since we stepped through the doors. "I very much doubt it was nothing, *reginetta*. It never is with you."

"Fine," Amalia says, smirking. "We were discussing the best escape routes and which ones take you the longest to run. But apparently, she doesn't want to escape you. Good job on the ring, by the way. It's lovely."

"Thank you. May I have a moment with my wife?"

She pops up from the sofa, turning a smile on Finley. "We'll talk later."

"Of course. Thank you, Amalia."

Amalia smiles at Finley, then sticks her tongue out at me before slipping from the room.

"Was she really telling you about her escape routes out of the house?"

"Yes." Finley laughs quietly. "She has a lot of them, doesn't she?"

"You have no idea. Coda and I chased her ass all over this fucking property when Rafe first brought her here. As soon as our backs were turned, she was gone. Why was she telling you about them?"

"She said every woman should get to decide for herself where she wants to be. I guess she wanted to make sure that I was really with you by choice and not because I didn't feel like I had no other option." She smiles. "I think it was a test."

"For you or me?"

"Both?" She shrugs. "I'm not sure, but I think we passed."

"That's good." I pace to the window, staring out.

"If you're stressing out about telling me that I have to go meet my uncle, I already know," she says softly, stepping up behind me. "I figured that out before we ever left the safehouse, Domani."

"Cazzo." I spin to face her. "I don't want to take you."

"I know, but you have no choice. Neither of us do."

"I won't let him touch you." I press my fingers to her cheek. "I won't let him hurt you, *mio sole*."

"I know." She pushes her way into my arms, burrowing into me. "Promise me something, Domani?"

"Anything."

"When this is over, we'll go back to your cabin and pretend the rest of the world doesn't exist for a little while. I just want to be with you. No one else."

"I'll take you anywhere you want to go, *tesoro*. Anywhere."

"To paradise, Domani. I just want to go back to paradise."

Fifteen minutes later, I dial the number that texted me this morning. Finley grips my hand as if she's never going to let it go. Rafe and Mattia sit on the opposite side of his desk, watching.

"It took you long enough to call," Cillian says as soon as he answers. I've never spoken to him, but I know by the way Finley's hand tightens around mine that it's him.

"I didn't see you picking up the phone, either."

"Are we making a trade or not?"

"I want to speak to Coda first."

"That's not on the table."

"It is if you ever want to see your niece again," I taunt. "Because we aren't trading jackshit until I know that he's alive and well."

"Fine." A rustling comes down the line.

"Hey, brother," Coda says. He sounds like shit, but he's alive.

"Hey. Do you remember the night the *reginetta* came into our lives? You said something after we met her for the first time. What did you say, brother?"

"*Donna buona val più d'una corona.*"

"Yeah," I say softly. "A good woman is worth more than a crown." He's alive, then. This isn't some trick or recording Cillian is trying to pass off as the real thing. Coda is still breathing. Now, we need to keep him that way. "We're coming for you, brother. Just hang tight."

"I want to talk to my niece," Cillian demands.

I nod to Finley, silently reminding her that I'm right here. We knew he'd want to hear from her and that she'd have to convince him that I've been holding her against her will.

"Hi, Uncle Cillian," she says, her voice shaking like a leaf.

I exhale a tiny breath when I hear it. I fucking hate that she's scared. But the fact that she is works in our favor. For all he knows, she's terrified because I have her, not because she's speaking to him. As far as he knows, she was taken against her will. He has no real reason to believe that she was trying to escape. She's always been obedient, always played along with his rules. He tied her up simply to remind her that he could.

"Finley. We've been worried about you. Are they treating you well?"

"Yes, uncle," she whispers. "I want to go home."

"Soon, *a leanbh.*"

"That's enough," I growl, ending the conversation before she has to say anything else and risks saying too much. "If you want her back, I want Coda. And then you walk the fuck away. No bullshit."

"No bullshit? You're the one who came into my home and took my niece," he growls. "I'm the wronged party here."

"We both know everything about you is wrong, Brennan. Including your presence in this city. You're here because we allow you to be here. Don't push us. If you want her back, you'll be at the storage facility at the harbor at midnight."

"Is this the part where you tell me to come alone?" he asks, cold amusement lacing his voice.

"I don't care who you bring. If you're such a coward that you need to surround yourself with an army to make the trade, then by all means, be a fucking coward. But be there at midnight, or you'll never see her alive again." I disconnect without giving him an opportunity to say anything else.

"*Cristo*, Domani," Rafe growls. "Did you have to taunt him? The last thing we need is for him to show up with a goddamn army."

"Weak men will do anything to avoid looking weak," I murmur, lifting Finley out of her chair into my lap. I don't care who is watching. My wife needs comfort, and I'll provide it. "He won't bring an army. He knows it's what we expect."

"You better hope you're right. Because we'll be split down the middle."

Chapter Fourteen

Finley

The storage facility at the harbor is a massive complex housing countless dozens of shipping crates. It's a maze unless you know where you're going. Domani, Mattia, and Rafe seem to know exactly where they're going as they lead me through the maze, heading toward some building they claim is on the far side.

Several of Rafe's men have scattered throughout the complex, taking up positions to help keep an eye out. They're our backup. Luca, Diego, and a man named Alessio are on the way to my uncle's house along with the rest of Rafe's men. At exactly fifteen minutes after midnight, they'll make entry, killing everyone they come across.

Gabriel is back at the mansion with their wives, responsible for protecting them with his life. I don't think Rafe or Luca wanted him involved. I get the sense that he's in this life only by necessity. He doesn't fit like the others do. There's a shadow over him, as if the things he does for this family cost him greatly. I think maybe they might. But he does them anyway because there's not much he wouldn't do for those he loves.

The smell of the water is strong here. So is the stench of oil. The combination makes my stomach churn. Or perhaps that's simply the fact that in an hour, my uncle will be here. One way or another, this will be over.

I'll either be permanently in heaven or sentenced to hell.

I've never cared for the heat.

"This one," Rafe says, stopping suddenly.

Mattia and Domani stop too. I glance at my husband, not sure why they seem to know what Rafe is talking about, but I don't.

"Thanks," Domani says.

Rafe nods and then he and Mattia continue on, leaving me and Domani alone.

"What's going on?" I ask.

"Do you think you can remember this crate, *mio sole*?" he asks.

I glance at it, brows furrowed. It looks like all the others. It's bright blue and massive. There are dozens more just like it. "I don't know. Why?"

"Because this crate never moves. It's been here for years, hiding an emergency access hatch to the drainage system below the harbor," he says. "It's dark and wet, but the system lets out all over the city. Everyone has forgotten this access exists."

"Everyone except Rafe."

"Yes."

"He doesn't forget much, does he?"

"No, he doesn't. He's held onto this entire complex because of this hatch." Domani taps the side of the crate. "It's been useful."

"In what way?"

He meets my gaze.

"Oh," I whisper, reading the truth on his face. They use it to move bodies. I guess the water here holds more than just the trash and pollution the people of Chicago have dumped into it. I suppose it's better than choking the city with the smell of their burning flesh, but it's gruesome in its own right.

"I need you to remember this crate, *tesoro*. If anything goes wrong, you have to make your way back here. This is how you'll get out of here."

"Domani, I'm not leaving without you."

"You will," he says, pressing his finger to my lips. "If it comes down to it and it's my life or yours, you choose yours, Finley. I need you to promise."

"I can't."

"You can."

"If he gets his hands on you, you'll beg for death, *mio sole*. The life you lived before is gone. He'll never let you go back to that. Not once he realizes that you chose us. He'll torment you every day just because he can. Just because that's the type of monster he is. I can't let you go back to that. You have to promise that, no matter what, if it comes down to a choice between saving my life or ending up back in his hands, you'll run."

"Domani," I cry, tears welling up and spilling over. "I don't want to make this promise."

"I know you don't, *tesoro*. But I can't do what I need to do until I know that, no matter what, you'll fight like hell to stay out of his hands. You don't belong in a cage. I need you to decide right now that you're never going back to one. I can't make the choice for you. Only you get to decide what you're willing to allow." He brushes the tears from my cheeks, touching his forehead to mine. "You have to set yourself free, *amore mio*."

He's right, damn him. He carried me out of my uncle's house, but he can't set me free. Only I can do that. I'm the only one who can take back the piece of me still trapped in that fucking house, held hostage by terror.

"Fine," I whisper, one piece of my heart breaking while another heals. "I'll do it, Domani. If it comes down to do it, I'll leave you there to keep him from getting his hands on me." I pull back to meet his gaze. "And I'll spend the rest of my life mad as hell at you for leaving me here alone.

I'll never forgive you for it." My bottom lip quivers. "And I'll never stop loving you."

"*Tesoro*." He dips his head, claiming my mouth in a hard kiss. He pours everything into it. His heart. His soul. His fierce pride. He gives me everything he has and everything he is, holding nothing back.

I taste my tears on our lips, seasoning our kiss with pain. In this life, we only know happiness because of pain. So it's fitting, I suppose, that the taste of my tears makes the joy of his kiss all that much sweeter.

"*Ti amo*," he whispers.

"You and me forever," I whisper back.

My uncle and Cian arrive half an hour later with four of their men in tow. It's far fewer than I expected he'd bring. They have tape over Coda's mouth, and his hands are bound behind his back. Even tied up, he's far more powerful than my uncle could ever hope to be, towering over him like a veritable giant.

My uncle tops out at five-nine. He's short, with crew-cut red hair and icy blue eyes. He's handsome in his own way...if you can look past the fact that he's a complete psycho. Cian looks just like him, though he's several inches taller and stockier.

I've never seen the four men with them. They seem uneasy about being here now. I don't think they're entirely on board with taking on Rafe Valentino and his family. The man's reputation precedes him. From what little I know, everyone in this city walks softly in Rafe Valentino's presence. Apparently, that includes my uncle's cronies.

But my uncle has always had an unquenchable thirst for power. I've always wondered if he was the one who killed my dad in a bid to claim his throne.

They never caught who did it. His death has always been a big question mark in my mind. For a long time, I refused to even consider that Cillian might have had something to do with it. But that was before he moved me to Chicago and kept me locked up in that house, claiming it was for my own good. That was before I listened to him rape and murder and destroy.

Would he kill his own brother? Yes, he would. But did he? I don't think I'll ever know. He'll never tell me.

My hands shake as he and Cian stalk toward us across the concrete floor of the warehouse. I'm sitting in a chair, my hands behind me as if they're tied. They aren't, but he doesn't know that.

"Valentino," he growls to Rafe.

"Brennan."

Cillian flicks a dismissive gaze at Mattia and then turns those cold eyes on Domani. "Brambilla."

"Brennan."

"I want my fucking niece."

"Send Coda over, and you can have her."

"No. Coda stays here. She stays there. We swap sides," Cillian says. "No bullshit."

It's not ideal. It puts him far closer to me than I know Domani wants to risk. But he isn't getting out of here alive. I can practically read Domani's thoughts. I feel his rage. My uncle hasn't even looked at me since he walked into the warehouse, and Domani is livid about it.

I'm not in the least surprised. Cillian doesn't care about me. He isn't concerned about my safety or welfare. He's simply pissed that Domani took me from him. That's all he cares about...the fact that something that he believes belongs to him was taken.

Well, I have bad news for him. I don't belong to him. I never will. I belong to Domani. I always have. Even before I met him, my soul was his to take. Since the moment I was put on this earth, I've belonged to him, and he's belonged to me.

But Cillian wouldn't understand that. He doesn't even have a soul. He sure as hell doesn't know how to love.

"Fine," Domani growls. "Just get the fuck on with it. We've got more important shit to do."

Everyone steps forward at the same time. I hold my breath, terrified of what the next few seconds will bring. I already know it comes with a hail of bullets and death. I just hope it's not Domani's death. Or Rafe's. Or Mattia's. Or my own.

No one says anything as they close the distance between each other. The tension in the warehouse is so thick I could cut it with the knife clutched in my shaking hands. The gap between them shrinks smaller and then smaller.

They pass by each other. Cillian and Cian are on my side of the warehouse now, moving closer. My uncle reaches into his waistband. I see the gun hidden there.

"Gun!" I scream at Domani, warning him of what's about to happen.

Cillian looks at me now. His cold eyes flash to me, full of malice. Full of shock.

That's right, asshole. You don't own me.

"You little bitch," he roars.

Domani and Rafe spin, their guns already in their hands.

I throw myself out of my chair, landing on my side on the floor.

The first shots rip through the warehouse. Cian doesn't even have a chance to pull his weapon. He doesn't even have a chance to turn around. His blood splatters everywhere as he falls.

Cillian roars in rage, shooting wildly in my direction. Domani plows into him from behind. I scream as they hit the floor and go rolling, fists flying. Another bullet ricochets off the floor beside my head. I sob, scrambling backward.

One of Cillian's men runs after me. Rafe and Mattia are busy with the other three, exchanging potshots, and Coda is still trying to free himself from the rope tying his hands together. I swing the knife wildly, trying to keep the man away from me.

He's a lot bigger and a lot faster than I am, though. And he's on his feet, not on his butt on the floor. He has every advantage. He grabs a handful of my hair, dragging me backward.

I lash out with the knife again, barely missing him.

"Let me go!"

"Fuck no."

I try to stab him again and miss him again. Maybe Domani should have been teaching me how to use this stupid knife instead of fucking me all week because I'm useless right now.

The man laughs, pulling my hair tighter.

I scream in fury and in pain, flipping myself around to face him. He doesn't expect that. The knife sinks into his thigh. I yank downward, ripping his thigh open.

"You bitch!" he roars, trying to backhand me across the face.

I duck the blow, jabbing him in the shin with the knife.

He kicks me off of him. I manage to get a glimpse of Domani and my uncle. They're still rolling around on the floor. Domani rolls on top of my uncle, punching him in the face. He hits him so hard he loses his center of balance. My uncle immediately throws him off, trying to grab the gun a few feet away.

My attacker grabs me by the throat, and I lose track of my husband and my uncle.

"I should fucking kill you right here and now," the man growls in my ear. "You're worth more to us dead than you are alive anyway."

"No, I'm not," I rasp, struggling to keep the knife out of his hands. "I'm married now. If he kills me, my trust fund goes to my husband. He'll never touch my money again. Not now, not ever."

The confession does exactly as I wanted. It shocks him just enough to distract him. He loosens his grip momentarily, allowing me to yank free of it. I slash out with the knife, catching him across the back of the arm as I propel myself to my feet, preparing to run.

Coda looms up in front of me like a wall. I bounce off of his chest, nearly landing on my ass on the floor all over again. He catches me with his hands around my arms and quickly shuffles me to the side, his gaze locked on the man pursuing me.

"Run, *piccola*."

I don't listen. Of course I don't. Coda crashes into my attacker like a tsunami hitting the coast. I let him have at it, frantically searching for Domani and Cillian. They're several feet from where I last saw them, still rolling around. Cillian may be half Domani's size, but he's been boxing his entire life. He's a fighter. He knows hand-to-hand and how to protect himself.

But Domani knows what he's doing too. They're evenly matched, neither getting the upper hand. Both delivering brutal, punishing blows. They're both bleeding. I think my uncle may be bleeding more than Domani, but blood drips from cuts on his face, too.

"You locked her in that fucking house!" he roars at my uncle, wrapping his hands around his throat. "You forced her to listen to every sick, twisted thing you did, you piece of shit."

My uncle bucks him off. "She'll keep listening," he growls. "Long after you're fucking rotting in the ground, she'll lay in her bed at night and listen to what I do in the room down the hall. Maybe I'll even force her to watch this time."

Domani roars, leaping on him again. My uncle is prepared for his attack, though. He flips him onto his back, bashing his head against the concrete floor.

I cry out in horror at the sickening sound. It's so loud.

My eyes land on the gun they were fighting for earlier. I scurry forward and grab it, though I have no idea how to use it. I sob, trying to figure it out, desperate to help Domani before Cillian kills him. Only to realize there's no need.

Domani grabs Cillian by the throat, slamming him to the floor. He hauls himself on top of him, bleeding from a gash across the back of his head. But he's too pissed to be slowed or stopped now. My uncle threatened me, and that's the one thing he shouldn't have done. My husband can't be stopped now. He has no mercy.

He hits my uncle again and again, his fist connecting with his face as blood splatters and bone crunches. "You'll never touch her again, you motherfucker!" he roars. "She'll never step foot in that fucking house. She's mine, and hell will freeze over before you get anywhere near her ever again."

He hits my uncle a final time and then slams him back to the ground. My uncle doesn't move this time. He simply lays there, defeated.

Domani climbs off him, swaying on unsteady legs. He wheels around, searching wildly for me. As soon as his eyes land on me, the rage in his expression cools. He relaxes slightly, as if drawing his first deep breath in hours.

"Come here, *mio sole*," he says, his voice so much softer than it was just a moment ago. He speaks to me with reverence and devotion. With respect. There was nothing but implacable fury and hard malice when he spoke to my uncle. These are the two sides of my husband, I realize. The gentle man he is only for those he loves and the deadly, dangerous monster that cracks his eyes open and comes out to play when called.

I hurry to him, embracing both sides. Loving both sides.

He buries his face in my hair, breathing me in.

"We made it," I wish. "It's over."

"Not yet, *tesoro*. He's still alive."

I lift my gaze to Domani's, searching.

"You have another choice to make," he says quietly. "You can walk out of here right now and I'll pull the trigger for you. He'll die, and you'll be free. You'll never have to worry about him ever again."

"What's my other option, Domani?"

"You know it already." He nods at the gun in my hand. "It's the reason you picked that up, *mio sole*. If you want to slay your own dragon, no one here will judge you for it. No one here will ever breathe a word of it, either."

I stand silently for a moment, weighing my choices. No matter which I pick, I know this man will continue to love me. He won't see me any differently or judge me. Whether I pull the trigger or not, he'll still look at me exactly the same. I don't need to kill him myself to be free, though. I already am. But there is one thing I do need. "I need to ask him something before I make my choice," I say quietly.

Domani strides toward him, kicking him in the ribs. "Wake up," he barks when my uncle groans. "Your niece has a question for you. How quickly we put you out of your misery depends on how honestly you answer. Lie to her and I'll keep you alive until you beg for death. Tell her the truth, and I'll let you go now."

"Fuck you," Cillian spits.

"No, fuck you, Cillian," Rafe says, stepping up beside Domani. "You've already lost. Your sons are dead. Her money is gone. She's got his ring on her finger, and if he's lucky, his kid is growing in her belly. Chicago is mine. I'll root out every single one of your fucking people if that's what I have to do. And I'll keep you alive, torturing you every fucking day while I do it if you don't answer her goddamn question."

Cillian spits again, blood running down his chin. "Ask it," he growls.

Domani holds out a hand to me, calling me forward.

I slip mine into his, letting him ground me as I stare down at the uncle who caused so much grief, turmoil, and pain in my life. Even now, he's a monster. He'll always be a monster. But I'm not afraid of him any longer.

"Did you kill him, Cillian?" I ask. "Were you the one who planted the car bomb that killed my dad?"

He rolls his eyes toward me. The left one is swollen nearly shut. The right one is bruised. But I see the regret and guilt in them, and I have my answer. He killed his own brother. He murdered my father.

As it turns out, the gun isn't as difficult to use as I thought. All it takes is the proper motivation. The blast rips through the warehouse.

Cillian jerks as the bullet sinks into his groin.

I drop the gun and step back.

"Kill him," I whisper, walking away.

Chapter Fifteen

Domani

"Is it over?" Finley asks, lifting her gaze to me as I climb into the back of the SUV beside her. She's exhausted and pale.

"Yeah, *tesoro*," I murmur, dragging her across the seat into my arms. "It's over." Luca called while we were weighing down their bodies. Everyone at the house is dead. Cillian's foothold in Chicago is gone. And so is he.

A bullet to the head ended his miserable life. But I let him bleed out for a while first. Just to make sure he had a little time to regret the choices he's made. I think part of him did, at least some of them anyway. Like killing his brother.

I hope he rots in hell with regret eating him for eternity.

It's less than he deserves for everything he's put her through. But he's done tormenting her now. He'll never hurt her again. No one will. I'll spend my entire life ensuring it.

That's my job now. Not hunting monsters but protecting this woman from them. She's my purpose. She's my reason. And she's my salvation. Somewhere along the way, she became my healer too. My wounds don't bleed like they once did. My father's crimes don't haunt me like they have for most of my life. She gave me peace when I've never had that.

I didn't even realize it had happened until today. Until I stood across from Cillian and realized that urge to hunt and punish had died. All I wanted to do was protect, defend, and ensure he could never hurt again. That's my mission now.

God can sort out the rest.

"Then take me home, Domani," Finley says, laying her head against my chest. "Take me back to paradise like you promised."

"Anything you want, *amore mio*," I murmur. "Anything at all."

"Easy. You and me forever. That's what I want."

"Then it's yours, Finley. *Io e te per sempre.*"

"I love you, Domani."

I rest my lips against her crown, already in paradise. Every time she says those words, she takes me there. I doubt she'll ever stop. Fifty years from now, she'll say it, and I'll still feel the same way.

That's what it is to be complete.

That's what it is to belong to her, body and soul.

"Ti amo, tesoro. Ti amo."

Epilogue

Finley

Five Years Later

"Wake up, *tesoro*," Domani murmurs, slipping his hand between my legs to stroke my clit. His lips brush across my shoulder as he pulls my leg back, hitching it over his hip from behind. His erection nudges at my entrance, hard and insistent. "Wake up."

"Mmm," I moan, pushing my ass back against him. "I'm not sleeping.

"Little liar," he chuckles.

"I'm resting my...Oh god." He sinks into me, stealing the familiar words as my body stretches around him, welcoming him. Pleasure billows through me in a soft wind, hot and stiff.

He rocks into me in steady pulses, making love to me slowly, sweetly. One hand runs all over my body. The other plays between my legs. It's heaven. With him, it's always heaven. This is my favorite way to wake up. With him already between my legs. Sometimes, he's eating me. Sometimes, he's touching me. Other times, he's already fucking me. I belong to him, my body his to take. I never tell him no. He doesn't deny me, either.

We're two sides of the same coin, as tangled up in each other as ever. More in love, more obsessed, and greedier every single day. We sneak away often for moments like this, for days at the cabin or time alone. Sometimes, we bring the kids with us. Sometimes, we leave them with our nanny. We never stay long without them. I can't go more than a night without seeing our babies. But I need moments like this, too. Days when it's just me and Domani, wrapped up in each other, fucking until we're as sated as we can be.

This is my happy place. This is my heaven. Right here in his arms, with him thrusting into me, his hands on my body, nothing in between us. This is where I belong. I've never felt freer than I do when I'm in his arms.

I've never been freer than I am at his side.

He wraps his hand around my throat, anchoring me in place as his thrusts grow harder and deeper. His teeth sink into my shoulder.

I cry out, sobbing his name into the room.

"Louder, *mio sole*," he demands. "Louder."

I shout it over and over, loving the sound of it on my lips. Domani. Domani. Domani. I could say it for eternity and never grow tired. I could love him for a thousand lifetimes and still want more. I am obsessed with this man. Completely. Utterly, Irrevocably.

My heart is his. My soul is his. Everything I am belongs to him.

I shatter apart, crying his name into the room. He groans, following me over the edge. We don't separate. We don't even stop fucking, not really. We just pause for a moment to catch our breath.

"*Ti amo*," he whispers, turning my face toward his to kiss my lips.

"I love you," I breathe.

He smiles, and I find another reason to love him. That smile. Just like the one before. And the one before that.

Author's Note

Thanks so much for reading Domani and Finley's story. If you enjoyed their book, please consider leaving a review.

Next in this series is Coda's book, Irredeemable. It is now available for pre-order.

Need to catch up with the Valentino family? The Ruined series (Nico, Rafe, Luca, and Gabriel's books) is available here. You can also find Diego's book here.

Irrevocable (Domani's story): mybook.to/DomaniNR – Out Now

Irredeemable (Coda's story); mybook.to/CodaNR – Coming in April

Irreplaceable (Mattia's story): mybook.to/MattiaNR – Coming in June

Redemption never hurt so good.

For years, the dark and delicious Valentino brothers have ruled the city of Chicago with closed fists and iron wills. They're ruthless, merciless, and wicked. But even kings fall. And the curvy women meant for them are about to drop these crime bosses to their knees. But not before these obsessed mafia men strip them of every single defense they have.

Mercy is for the weak. These curvy girls are about to learn what it means to beg.

Physical Science (Nico and Norah) – One twin wants to kill her. The other wants to worship her. When the dust settles, will love prove triumphant for the curvy young student caught between the professor of her dreams and the dangerous mob boss who haunts her nightmares? Prequel novella.

Wrecked (Rafe and Amalia) – In a city where crime doesn't sleep, Rafe Valentino is a waking nightmare. But even kings fall. And this king promises to leave behind a crater when he falls for the curvy sister of his enemy. But she's keeping secrets that just might burn his empire to the ground with him. Will the powerful connection between them survive the truth, or will his enemies use it to destroy them both?

Wanton (Luca and Callandria) – A life in hell was the sacrifice Luca Valentino made to keep his brothers alive. And there's nothing he won't do to see the job through...even if it means seducing the enemy. But he never intended to fall for her. Now, the woman who holds the key to his future is in chains in his bedroom, and their families are on the brink of war.

Wicked (Gabriel and Genesis) — They say those with the power make the rules...but when Gabriel Valentino meets Genesis Burbank, the rules go out the window. The curvy bombshell refuses to bend to his will, and he isn't used to losing. Especially when it matters. He'll do whatever it takes to possess her. Even if he has to break her to claim her.

Ruined: The Complete Series is out now.

Follow Nichole

Like free books? Me too! Sign-up for my mailing list at http://authornicholerose.com/newsletter to stay up-to-date on all new releases and for exclusive giveaways and freebies!

Want to connect with me and other readers? Join Nichole Rose's Book Beauties on Facebook!

Grab signed copies of books, book boxes, and more at http://nicholerose.shop.

facebook.com/AuthorNicholeRose/

instagram.com/AuthorNicholeRose

twitter.com/AuthNicholeRose

bookbub.com/authors/nichole-rose

tiktok.com/@authornicholerose

Nichole's Book Beauties

Want to connect with Nichole and other readers? We're building a girl gang! Join Nichole Rose's Book Beauties on Facebook for fun, games, and behind-the-scenes exclusives!

The Instalove Book Club is now in session!

Get the inside scoop from your favorite instalove authors, meet new authors to love, and snag a free book and bonus content from featured authors every month. The Instalove Book Club newsletter goes out once per week!

Join the Club: http://instalovebookclub.com

Also by Nichole Rose

Find links to my books, audiobooks, the suggested reading order, and a downloadable map of how books connect on my website at http://authornicholerose. com!

Her Alpha Series
Her Alpha Daddy Next Door
Her Alpha Boss Undercover
Her Alpha's Secret Baby
Her Alpha Protector
Her Date with an Alpha
Her Alpha: The Complete Series

Her Bride Series
His Future Bride
His Stolen Bride
His Secret Bride
His Curvy Bride

His Captive Bride

His Blushing Bride

His Bride: The Complete Series

Claimed Series

Possessing Liberty

Teaching Rowan

Claiming Caroline

Kissing Kennedy

Claimed: The Complete Series

Love on the Clock Series

Adore You

Hold You

Keep You

Protect You

Love on the Clock: The Complete Series

The Billionaires' Club

The Billionaire's Big Bold Weakness

The Billionaire's Big Bold Wish

The Billionaire's Big Bold Woman

The Billionaire's Big Bold Wonder

The Billionaires' Club: The Complete Series

<u>Playing for Keeps</u>

Cutie Pie

Ice Breaker

Ice Prince

Ice Giant

Cold as Ice

Ice Storm

Playing for Keeps: The Complete Series

<u>Full-Length Titles</u>

Crash into You

Fight for You (coming soon)

Kill for You (coming soon)

<u>The Second Generation</u>

A Blushing Bride for Christmas

<u>Love Bites</u>

Come Undone

Dripping Pearls

<u>Echoes of Forever</u>

His Christmas Miracle

Taken by the Hitman

Wicked Saint

<u>The Ruined Trilogy</u>

Physical Science

Wrecked

Wanton

Wicked

Ruined: The Complete Series

<u>Illicit Love Series</u>

Irresistible

Irrevocable

Irreplaceable

Irredeemable

<u>Destination Romance</u>

Romancing the Cowboy

Beach House Beauty

Pretty Little Mess

Hitched to the Heartthrob

<u>Standalone Titles</u>
A Touch of Summer
Black Velvet
His Secret Obsession
Dirty Boy
Naughty Little Elf
Tempted by December
Devil's Deceit
A Bride for the Beast (writing with Fern Fraser)
A Hero for Her
Dear Mr. Dad Bod

<u>Easy on Me</u>
Easy Ride
Easy Surrender

<u>One Night with You</u>
Falling Hard
Model Behavior
Learning Curve
Angel Kisses

Carmichael Security Series
Truly Mine

Madly Yours

Deeply Hers

Valkyrie Bound
Valkyrie Heart

Valkyrie Fate

Silver Spoon MC
The Surgeon

The Heir

The Lawyer

The Prodigy

The Bodyguard

Silver Spoon MC Collection: Nichole's Crew

Silver Spoon Falls
Xavier's Kitten

Callum's Hope

Snow's Prince

Aurora's Knight

<u>Silver Spoon Falcons</u>

Leia's Playmaker

Aspen's Defense

Gabbi's Goalie

Silver Spoon After Dark

Bound by Bronx

Coming for Coby

Daddy for Davina

<u>writing with Loni Ree as Loni Nichole</u>

Dillon's Heart

Razor's Flame

Ryker's Reward

Zane's Rebel

Oral Arguments

Grizz's Passion

Garrett's Obsession

The Daddy Claus

Submitting to Slade

About Nichole Rose

Three-time award-winning author Nichole Rose writes filthy romance for curvy readers. Her books feature headstrong, sassy women and the alpha males who consume them. From grumpy detectives to country boys with attitude to instalove and over-the-top declarations, nothing is off-limits.

Nichole is sure to have a steamy, sweet story just right for everyone. She fully believes the world is ugly enough without trying to fit falling in love into a one-size-fits-all box.

When not writing, Nichole enjoys fine wine, cute shoes, and everything supernatural. She is happily married to the love of her life and is a proud mama to the world's most ridiculous fur-babies. She and her husband live in Arkansas.

You can learn more about Nichole and her books at authornicholerose.com.

facebook.com/AuthorNicholeRose/

instagram.com/AuthorNicholeRose

twitter.com/AuthNicholeRose

bookbub.com/authors/nichole-rose

tiktok.com/@authornicholerose